LIBERTY BOY

David M. Gaughran is Irish but lives in Portugal these days, somewhere north of Lisbon in a lovely little fishing village. He likes dogs, whiskey, collecting old records, laborious puns, and also cooking elaborate feasts and inviting exactly nobody around to share them. He is also fond of slow cars, fast walks on the beach, movies which contain some form of time-loop, and any kind of song with a call-and-response element. When not busy learning everything he can about guillotines, he writes historical adventures like *Liberty Boy*, *Mercenary*, and *A Storm Hits Valparaiso*, as well as science fiction and writer guides under another name. Visit DavidGaughran Books.com to get a free novel. "Sure, why not?" says you.

Praise for *Liberty Boy:*

"*Liberty Boy* is a riveting tale of an overlooked rebellion, told from the perspective of the streets, with gifted dialogue that is more heard than read and unexpected twists that leave you breathless from first page to last."

—Cindy Vallar, *Historical Novel Society Review*.

Praise for *Mercenary:*

"Highly recommended to readers of adventure fiction and history, as well as anyone interested in American adventurism and meddling in Latin America."

—*Wall Street Journal* and *USA Today* bestselling author Michael Wallace.

"Lee Christmas led a roaring life on and off the battlefield. Gaughran's great, fast-paced read keeps you right alongside all his exploits."

—Richard Sutton, author of *The Red Gate*.

Praise for *A Storm Hits Valparaiso:*

"An ambitious story of love and betrayal, victory and defeat. In characters drawn from real historical figures, the author delves into the politics of war and how battles turn on the smallest of details or the whims of a single man."

—JW Manus, author of *The Devil His Due.*

"A work of sweeping historical fiction that captivates and entertains ... engaging and richly textured."

—John D. Glass, author of *Legend of Zodiac.*

BOOK 1 IN THE *LIBERTY* SERIES

LIBERTY BOY

DAVID GAUGHRAN

LIBERTY BOY
ISBN-13: 978-91-87109-39-3

Editor: Karin Cox
Cover Design: Kate Gaughran
Second paperback edition published July 2020
DavidGaughranBooks.com

To Ivča, for the magic potion.

"*The poor people of Ireland are rising fast. You will shortly be as well off as the English who have meat and bread and ale, and so will you if you be quiet. But you will get nothing by rioting except starvation and the gallows.*"
George Nugent Reynolds
Address to the Common People of Leitrim.

1

I T WAS THE kind of morning that made him wonder if God hated the Irish. Rain hoored down from the sky, helped on by a biting wind from the east, soaking those gathered in front of St. Catherine's Church. The market traders would normally have been delighted to see such a crowd here on a Thursday morning, halfway down the long, wide stretch of Thomas Street. However, these people weren't here to haggle or to barter but to howl and spit and rent the air with their screams.

They were here for a hanging.

Jimmy O'Flaherty stood apart from the throng, leaning against the exterior of McCann's alehouse at the top of Dirty Lane, in full view of the spectacle that was about to unfold, gazing forlornly at the place where his stall should have been. The stage erected in its stead was bare, apart from the scaffold that loomed over an imposing wall of red-coated soldiers beneath. There must have been a hundred of them there, casting baleful glares at the assembled Dubliners from behind their guns and bayonets.

To Jimmy's left, in the direction of his flat on the corner of Meath Street, a whole company of cavalrymen were ready to charge should there be a surge towards the scaffold when the prisoner arrived to meet his fate. Their faces were curiously blank. Jimmy decided they must be officers: men who relied on codes and regulations to trample common folk, rather than gauche personal animus. But the level of caution was no surprise; the Castle had much to contend with today.

The whole of Thomas Street had turned out and many more besides. Not just the United Irish crowd and their sympathizers either—Jimmy could see a vicar in amongst them, remonstrating with a mounted officer who had been liberally using a cudgel to beat clear a path for his charge. On the other side of the swarm was Paulie Grogan, a fellow trader who normally cursed the rebels to any who would listen, but he too was enraged by this very public execution.

It wasn't that surprising, Jimmy supposed. In this part of Dublin, at least, Catholics and Protestants lived cheek-by-jowl. Dissenters too. It had been that way in The Liberties since the Huguenots arrived from France a hundred years before, fleeing persecution of their

Calvinist ways. A few returned home after the Edict of Versailles, but most stayed. And those who did felt sympathy for their Catholic brothers as they suffered under the Penal Laws.

Wolf-whistles greeted a sergeant who climbed the stage, his lip curling slightly as he surveyed the scene, St. Catherine's Church squatting behind him. He barked out an order, and his phalanx of men shifted left. A cabbage sailed through the air, landing just short of sergeant's mud-spattered boots. Half a dozen soldiers pushed into the crowd, not caring who felt their bayonets, and hauled out a boy who couldn't have been more than twelve or thirteen. Jimmy wondered how they'd spotted the diminutive cabbage-thrower in all that tumult, until he realized they likely didn't care whether they had the right person. It was about keeping order. By any means necessary.

Weeks of reprisals and riots had followed the failed Rising at the end of July. It was clear that the Castle was hoping to flush out the rest of the traitors, turn Thomas Street on its head and turn neighbors into informants, but that only served to galvanize support for the cause. It was a lesson the English never learned, Da used to say. Rebels were far more popular after they swung at the end of a rope. Sure, Robert Emmet couldn't get three hundred to turn up to his rebellion, and there were easily three thousand here this morning. There would be ten times that again by the time they finally got around to hanging the rebel leader himself, Jimmy figured.

He'd been apoplectic when he heard that the executions would take place here on Thomas Street. Business had only just begun returning to normal. Usually, hangings took place at Gallows Hill, near Kilmainham Gaol, beyond St. James' Gate at the western edge of the city. The odd execution still took place up by Misery Hill at the Liffey-mouth, especially if it was a pirate—the corpse displayed for all docking vessels to see, vermin crawling over one another in a race to pick the bones clean. But Robert Emmet's base had been here in The Liberties, and his doomed rebellion was launched from this very street. It was a brutal show of strength by the Crown, a reminder to the people who really ruled this city. And they would keep hanging until the jails were emptied of rebels.

Jimmy's thoughts were interrupted by someone tugging his arm. He turned, expecting to swat away a beggar boy, but his grimace turned to surprise when he saw a pretty girl panting in front of him. "Do you know who they're hanging today?" she asked, her eyes flashing with anger as she spoke, as if her question hid an accusation.

"I do," he replied. "A man called Edward Kearney."

She blessed herself, still catching her breath. Her face was somewhat familiar, but Jimmy couldn't place it.

"Lord have mercy on his soul," she said, turning to face the gallows.

Jimmy examined her surreptitiously. He guessed she was around the same age as him—nineteen, or perhaps a little younger, he could never tell with women, something which had gotten him in trouble before. She had a snub nose and a roundish face. Her hair, almost as dark as his own, had been pulled back with a velvet band but that only served to highlight her eyes all the more, a striking shade of emerald green. Jimmy almost jumped when she turned to him again. He quickly switched his gaze back to the gallows, hoping she hadn't noticed.

"Do I know you from somewhere?" When she turned his way, her bright green eyes seemed to be mocking him.

"I was wondering the same thing."

"I'm from Smithfield," she said, extending her hand. "And my name is Kitty Doyle."

"Jimmy O'Flaherty," he replied, awkwardly taking her hand, hoping she wouldn't notice his clammy palms. He tried to think of something else to say, something clever, but his mind was blank. Then she looked down at her hand and Jimmy realized he was still clutching it tightly. Mortified, he stammered an apology, but as Kitty turned away, he noticed her slight, playful hint of a smile again. He felt his pulse quickening and hoped his face hadn't reddened. His naturally smooth patter from years of dealing with customers always fell apart when he spoke to a pretty girl. Meeting one in the open, without his cart in front of him as a protective barrier, almost brought him out in hives. He desperately tried to think, but everything he conjured up sounded foolish. Jimmy watched her eyes scan the crowd, from one end to the other, until her gaze rested on the gallows once more and her pretty face darkened.

"Edward Kearney," she repeated.

Jimmy nodded.

A hardness replaced that dancing light in her eyes. "Anyone else?"

"Don't think so," he said, happy she was taking the initiative. "Not today, at least. But this is only the start of it."

"A terrible waste." She curled a stray wisp of hair behind her ear.

He watched the soldiers fan out, clearing a path for the arriving prisoner. "That's one word for it."

"What's the other?"

"The other what?" he asked, confused.

Her eyes narrowed. "The other word for it."

Jimmy sighed. How could he even begin to answer that question? He simply shook his head at the foolishness of it all. The '98 Rebellion should have taught the United Irish that no amount of passion or pride could best guns or cannon, and that farmers and cobblers were poor substitutes for trained soldiers. How could Ireland take on the might of the Crown? It was madness, one that had consumed his father, leading to his death five years ago on Vinegar Hill. Jimmy was only fourteen back then—deemed too young for battle, despite his unending protestations. Da had waivered briefly, but Ma was immovable. She was the only reason he was still alive. They said his father wasn't killed in battle at all, but butchered by the Militia as he surrendered, along with thousands more. He felt his heart quicken as he thought of all that waste, so many lives thrown away for nothing.

"Kearney," the girl said, bringing him back to the present. "Did you know him?"

"Not very well. He dealt in skins, and I have a stall here at The Glib, so I'd see him around, but that's about the sum of it."

She stared at him a moment. "You don't sound like you have a lot of sympathy for the poor man."

"Aye, well…" He stared at the scaffold, struggling to order his thoughts.

"No one deserves to die like this," she said with some venom, and a little too loudly for Jimmy's liking.

He grabbed her by the elbow and leaned in closer. "I didn't mean it like that," he hissed. "Don't be getting me into trouble. There's been enough of that these last few months. Militia kicking down doors, dragging innocent people out of their beds. Thomas Street shut down while they searched the whole place for arms. Now there's talk of a whole fortnight of this shite."

"Shite?" Kitty balled her fists on her hips. "Selfish bastard!" She turned and gestured at the scaffold. "Sorry you have been *inconvenienced* by all this. Perhaps you should write a letter to the Castle."

Jimmy winced as Kitty emphasized the last words and several heads turned his way. He was relieved when she stormed off. Tempers were short around here these days. A stray word could earn a fella a box before he knew it was coming. He immediately regretted engaging that girl, despite her prettiness; she was clearly worked up about something. But his own fuse was short these days too. His family had held onto their spot at The Glib through thick and thin, but these last few weeks had almost finished them. The Corporation had offered all traders a temporary spot in the Ormond Market, but those jackals across the river would never let a fella from The Liberties trade in peace. Besides, if he couldn't catch the farmers on their way into town, there was no point setting up anywhere at all. Without fresh skins to bring to the tanners, he would have to pay full price for the leather he sold to the craftsmen and bookbinders, which would eat up all his profit.

He took off his cap and ran his hands through his hair. It wasn't often that someone knocked him off his stride, but this girl had gotten to him. While she had a point, he always minded his own business; why should he suffer for the actions of others? At the very least, he shouldn't feel guilty for looking out for himself. It was the only thing keeping people alive these days.

In a foul mood now and figuring it wouldn't be improved by watching some poor unfortunate choking to death, he pushed off the wall and turned down Dirty Lane towards Bridgefoot Street and the River Liffey, pulling his cap down over his eyes. Instinctively, he spun when the crowd fell silent, just in time to see a black-clad figure climb the ladder. Despite everything, he found himself creeping back up towards the spectacle. He couldn't be sure from this distance, but it looked like the impossibly broad-shouldered figure of Tom Galvin—the

City Executioner. There had been talk of bringing another in from Wales to spare Galvin any retribution, but that might have just been a rumor put about to protect him. He watched as the hangman checked the rope, and thought of his poor father—run down and hacked to bits like a rabid dog. But perhaps even that terrible fate was better than dying like this, where the last memory anyone had of you was your face turning blue and piss running down your leg.

Jimmy watched the herring sellers nibble at the edges of the crowd as the pickpockets dove into the center. Pamphleteers hawked broadsides while priests doled out blessings. A ballad singer shooed away a drunkard until he realized nobody else was willing to give him coin. Two prostitutes marked out their respective territory, glaring at each other. The crowd itself was focused on the stage. Most were angry—there could be little doubt on that front—but others seemed to take it as some kind of sport. Some had even brought their children, holding them aloft so they wouldn't miss a single grim detail. He even saw two members of the gentry—too well dressed to be from here, with their high leather boots and fashionably tight buckskin breeches. He watched as those two heartless bastards laughed and shook hands, probably betting whether the poor sod would break down and cry, or scream for his mother.

Dublin was making a lunatic of him.

He had to leave before he did anything foolish. It was hard to recall now, but there had been a plan, back before all this madness erupted in July. Or a dream, to be more accurate. His cousin Donal had traveled to America a few years back and was set up now in New York, constantly imploring him to make the voyage across. It even seemed possible, for a time. Jimmy had been saving diligently before Ma took a turn for the worse over the summer. Now, he was stuck here, at least until he could turn things around. But there was no doing that while Thomas Street served as a gallows.

Cursing the bind he found himself in, Jimmy continued down towards the river. He was watching a pair of mudlarks pick their way through the filthy edges of the Liffey when the roar went up from Thomas Street. The ragged children looked up at him for a moment, eyes narrowing with suspicion, before they scuttled back under the overhanging privies. Jimmy bent his head and said a silent prayer for the departed soul of the executed man. Then he swore to get the hell out of Ireland.

THE SUN WAS setting when Jimmy arrived back at Thomas Street, the light blinding him as he looked west towards the gallows. He shooed a peddler away from the door of No. 44 and entered the building he and Ma shared with seven more families, all considerably larger than his. They had traded away their larger ground floor room for a smaller one, right up in the eaves of the front-gabled old Dutch Billy. It meant a significant reduction in rent, welcome now there was only him supporting the family, but it was a move Jimmy regretted once Ma's health worsened.

Her coughing fits needed little provocation these days, and she rarely left the room, not with all those flights of stairs. Although, in truth, she rarely left her bed now either. Her spirit seemed to be slipping away in tandem with her health. The new room wasn't as well ventilated either. The damp often grew so bad that the walls would sweat. The landlord kept promising to fix the place up, but he couldn't be trusted to do anything that cost him coin, and the inclement weather usually meant Jimmy could leave the window open only a crack, if that, when leaving for work.

When he reached the top of the stairs, he noticed that Ma had left the door unlocked again. Sighing, he entered the room quietly, in case she was dozing. Her eyes were shut, so Jimmy pulled off his sodden cap and hung it over the fire, before giving the embers a poke. As the fire warmed him, he picked at some peeling paint under the mantelpiece and a lump of plaster tumbled off the wall. He shook his head and placed the chalky hunk on the mantelpiece where his father's books had once proudly stood; they were long sold now, along with anything else of value.

"Is that you, son?" came Ma's voice, from the bed.

Jimmy walked over and leaned down to kiss her forehead. "Sure, who else would it be?" Taking a seat on the edge of the bed, he brushed the damp hair back from her face. "Unless you've a new fella you haven't told me about."

"Watch your mouth," Ma said, but there was no malice in it. The fire had sprung up somewhat, so Jimmy spread his coat out to dry. From the corner of his eye, he saw his mother smile to herself—something he didn't see enough these days. "You going out again?" she asked.

"In a bit."

She had curious expression, her lips pursed. "Hope it's not to see that young one you were arguing with today."

"How—?"

She waggled a finger. "Never you mind."

Jimmy never failed to be surprised by Ma's knack of knowing everyone's business, even though she spent most of her time confined to bed. He grinned. "You could get a job up at the Castle with your spying abilities."

"Don't even joke about that," she replied, and this time there was an edge to her voice.

"Sorry, Ma."

She hoisted herself up a little in the bed. "Did you get me a drop?"

"I did. But do you not want dinner first?"

"Nora brought me something earlier."

"Ah," said Jimmy, knowing how his mother liked to gossip with her sister. "So she's the one who saw me getting a tongue-lashing from that pretty girl."

His Ma drew her lips into a thin line and regarded her son coolly. "Nora never said she was pretty."

"Ma…"

"They're the ones you have to watch," she said, tapping her nose. "They'll feed you with strong drink and you'll end up in Hell with the rest of them. And I want my son with me in Heaven."

"I know, Ma."

Remembering the meat pies he'd picked up on the way home, Jimmy fished them from his overcoat pocket and carefully unwrapped the hankie protecting them from the damp. He took a plate from the sideboard and left the food in the center of the table. "They're here if you get hungry later."

The table, like the bed, was built for a bigger room, but Ma insisted on keeping it. Da had all the furniture made for their wedding, and she always said she'd rather chop it all up for firewood than sell it for a quarter of what it was truly worth. He ran his hand along the surface, surprisingly true after all these years.

"Where are you off to?"

"I won't be long. There's a letter from Donal." He glanced at his mother. "Hold on." His eyes narrowed. "If Nora was here, she'd have told you already."

A smile spread across Ma's lips. "Just making sure you're not hiding anything from your poor old mother."

"Ah, don't start."

"You were always such a secretive child." Her smile faded. "Never telling me anything. Me, your only mother."

"Don't get yourself worked up." Jimmy knew he'd never get out of here if she started getting sentimental. "Now, do you want that drop before I go?" She nodded, and Jimmy set the glass down on her bedside table, noticing her eyes had become watery. "Ma…"

She gripped his arm with unexpected strength. "You're a good son," she said. "Now go before I start crying, and hurry back with all the news. I love Donal's letters."

ON THE WAY home from his aunt's house on The Coombe, Jimmy stopped into The Talbot Inn and took a glass of porter and a candle into a quiet corner, away from the ballad singers. He chuckled as some fella cocked his head back to polish off his stout and fell right off the stool onto the floor behind him. As his companions' laughter subsided, a fiddle drifted in from the front room, soon joined by a tin whistle. The players were good, too, not just following the standard notes but adding their own embellishments to the reel, and the crowd was lapping it up. Jimmy was almost tempted to join them.

Instead, he took the envelope out of his pocket. Donal's letter from America had been full of the usual: breathless tales of impossibly tall buildings, strange fruits, and exotic foreigners from all corners of the earth, as well as ostentatious displays of wealth among the family he served, and their never-ending stream of important guests. Towards the end had come a message just for Jimmy, and he wanted to read it before he returned home to Ma.

Aside from his estranged cousin, Jimmy was the only member of the extended family who could read and write to any kind of standard—he had his father to thank for that extravagance—and he'd been communicating secretly with Donal for some time now, slipping his clandestine notes into the letters Nora had him write.

This particular message was much longer than usual. Normally, Donal dashed out a few lines in the margins of the letter itself, which Jimmy skipped when reading aloud to the rest, but this was an entire page. He'd only been able to hang on to the envelope by fooling Nora, telling her that Ma insisted on getting the whole thing read to her properly this time. Even then, he'd had to swear on the family bible that he'd bring it back first thing in the morning, so she could keep it safe with the rest.

The lie didn't sit easily. But he had no choice, not without explaining things that were better kept unsaid. He sipped his pint, settling into position and wiping the creamy head from his upper lip as he sought the correct page. Moving the candle closer, he squinted to read.

"Jimmy," it began, "make sure you're reading this

part alone." He took another sup. *Here it comes,* he thought. "As you might have guessed, I've been laying it on a bit thick in the letters back home. You know how it is, Ma worries. America is a wonderful place—don't get me wrong—and I'm delighted to hear that you want to come, I really am."

He sighed with relief, and then continued reading.

"But I haven't been fully truthful. I couldn't be. What I was saying about New York being full of opportunity is all true. That no one really cares what church you belong to is also true. Well, *almost* true. There are Englishmen here after all."

He chuckled until he read the next words. "But you should think twice about coming—at least on the free boat. It's not what you think. Not at all. You're better off finding the fare or not coming. Not with your mother. Let me explain."

Donal talked a little about the journey over—not as arduous as he had feared, but not ideal for Ma in her current condition either. Jimmy flipped the page, and the next bit stopped him cold. "The captain told us all along that we were bound for New York, but it was Philadelphia we landed in—inland, up some big river. The paying passengers were let off as soon as we arrived, but the rest of us were kept onboard without a single word to let us know what was happening. Then a load of rich types came onboard to haggle with the captain."

He'd drunk most of his stout already, without realizing. The call came from across the room. "Another?"

He approached the counter, and the barman's eyes went to the letter he was still clutching in his left hand. "Bad news?"

Jimmy knocked back the end of his glass and handed it over the counter. "Sure, when is it ever good?" He returned to his spot in the corner.

"We were livestock at the Rathfarnham fair," the letter continued. "They checked us over like we were beasts, enquired as to our habits, and then asked whether we had a wife back home. It could have been a lot worse. I was lucky to have my contract bought by a reasonable man in the end. But decent and all that he is, I still have to work seven poxy years to clear the debt."

Some drunkard bumped into Jimmy's table and almost knocked his pint over, spilling wax across the page. Jimmy shoved him in the direction of the bar and kept reading. "Believe me when I tell you that you're better off paying the fare—no matter what you have to do to get the money. And that's before you even consider your mother. These fellas have no heart at all. I saw them splitting up man and wife—whole families even—if there was coin to be made.

"Take my advice," Donal concluded, "pay the fare or don't come at all."

He stared at the final lines for some time before the barman caught his eye. Jimmy waved him away and folded the letter back in his pocket, and then he went back home to Ma.

2

A BLACK PIGLET ran right down the center of Thomas Street, chased the whole way by a bawling young girl with blonde plaits. Jimmy watched from the entrance of No. 44 as she caught up to the tiny pig and embraced it, falling over when she attempted to scoop it up. It sniffed the little girl's face as she continued to cry in the dirt, puzzling him until she was surrounded by a group of men carrying long butcher's knives. Eventually she was led away, still rubbing her eyes, while the squealing piglet was carried off in the opposite direction. Jimmy sighed and headed for St. Catherine's Church.

He glowered at that damned gallows, left up overnight and blocking off half the street; there would be no trading here today either. He hoped to God they wouldn't have another hanging tomorrow. Saturday was when he made half his takings for the week—all those country boyos swanning around with money in their pockets. Many of them had airs about them, complaining about the stink from all the breweries and distilleries off Thomas Street, as if they hadn't spent half their lives covered in pigshit.

Maybe he was used to it, but the smell never seemed too bad unless the wind was coming from the south, blanketing The Liberties in the pungent emanations from the Blackpitts tanneries, or unless it was unusually warm and the nightsoilmen hadn't cleared the dump at Mullinahack. That didn't stop the country lads putting on airs and graces, thrusting their noses into perfumed handkerchiefs that they'd likely only purchased that morning. Some of them farmboys would even risk a dig in the head by claiming the odors 'suited the general moral failings of the locals.' These very same farmers would later be packing the brothels of Hell, behind Christchurch, guzzling cheap gin and buying trinkets for their favorite whores.

"Oh, it's you," he heard, while looking to his boots for inspiration.

He glanced up to see Kitty Doyle, the hot-tempered lass from the day before. "Aye," he said, furrowing his brow. "It's me."

"Sorry about yesterday."

He waved a hand in response, figuring the fewer words the better with this one.

Kitty squirmed a little and then her green eyes turned to the empty scaffold, the noose swaying slightly in the breeze. "It's just…"

He was loath to say anything at all, instead choosing to watch as she struggled with her emotions, her chest heaving, breath quickening. When he realized he was gaping, he flushed and snapped his attention back to the scaffold. Suddenly, he realized why she'd approached him. "It's Thomas Maxwell Roach today," he said quietly.

"Thank you." She nodded, taking her leave.

Jimmy watched her walk away for a moment, before calling out, "but there's another trial later." Kitty turned and approached him hesitantly, her face lined with worry.

"I don't know whose, I'm afraid," he added. "Or whether there'll be another execution tomorrow."

"Thanks."

Jimmy could see the pain she was wrestling with. He felt for her. He tried to think of something comforting, without prying. "Tomorrow's a big market day," he ventured. "Maybe they'll leave it off for the weekend."

Her eyes flashed with anger. "Can't have you missing out on trade."

"That's not what I…" But it was too late. She was gone.

He continued staring in the direction she'd strode off in until he was shoved in the back. Jimmy spun on his heel, ready to give someone a puck in the jaw until he saw a redcoat in front of him. "Move back, Paddy." The soldier's narrowed eyes challenged him.

Jimmy met his stare for a moment before retreating to the other side of the street, calming himself with the reminder that this was their game: provoking a reaction. He cracked his knuckles as he stalked down Thomas Street, pausing at the top of Vicar Street when he spied Fergal Hayes—the closest thing Jimmy had to a friend, even if he was a bit of a prick. Jimmy also suspected he was a United man; he sympathized with the rebels at the very least. But Fergal was even more interested in making coin, which was where they found common ground.

"Where are you off to?" Fergal asked by way of greeting.

"Nowhere in particular," Jimmy admitted, slowing to a halt.

Fergal grabbed his elbow. "Come on then."

Jimmy followed him back towards the gallows without protest, although he wasn't keen on watching the execution, if that's what Fergal had in mind. Da had once brought him to one as a boy. It had been a woman, meaning they burnt the corpse after and the noose too—

a relic of the superstitious days when they'd burned witches, his father had theorized. Whatever the reason, Jimmy would never forget the sickly sweet smell of burning flesh, or the primal screams that issued from that poor woman. It was rare, these days, to see a woman hang. Usually, they were able to plead the belly and be spared death—even if they had to bribe a turnkey to knock them up.

"I know that look," said Fergal. "A man only looks that troubled when he's thinking about a woman."

Jimmy scowled.

"Fine." Fergal tapped his nose. "But I want *all* the details if you actually do more than just talk this time."

He'd once made the mistake of confessing to Fergal that he'd never lain with a woman. Shocked, Fergal had offered to take him to Hell that very night. Jimmy was even tempted, for a moment, until Fergal explained that his father had taken him down there at the age of fourteen to make a man out of him, upon which Jimmy's desire evaporated.

"What's got you today?"

"Oh, nothing," he replied. "Was just wondering if this lot would clear off after the show."

"Did you not see it yesterday?"

"I did, but I thought…" Jimmy spread his hands.

"Thought what? The novelty would wear off? This is going to get worse, not better. They're hanging the lower fellas first, hoping one of them will turn King's Evidence. Then the bigger fish. This is going to build and build."

"But what about the market?"

"Forget it until October."

"October?"

"At least."

Jimmy threw his hands up in despair.

"I have an idea," said Fergal.

"Don't say Newmarket. There's no point heading up there."

Fergal shook his head. "I was thinking something else altogether. The City Watch is down by St. James' Gate now, directing people down towards the Liffey."

"But once they head down there, we've lost them. The Ormond crew won't let us make money on their patch."

"Exactly. We need to get their business before they reach St. James' Gate."

He realized what Fergal was suggesting. "Let's go see."

"Don't want to wait for this?" He nodded toward the scaffold.

Jimmy shoved him in response. "Move!"

Once they were through St. James' Gate and beyond the bustling entrance to the Guinness brewery, he saw what Fergal meant. The Watch weren't exactly forcing the detour, but they were detaining anyone who wanted to enter Thomas Street for long enough that few bothered. All the rest turned down Watling Street, towards the Liffey and the markets of Smithfield on the opposite side of the river. He cursed and continued walking briskly down the curve of James' Street until they were out of sight. Around the bend, he stopped. A hundred yards ahead of them, right where the road forked, stood an imposing obelisk. Jimmy remembered his father bringing him down here when it was being built. He was only a child then, but he remembered the scene quite clearly: workmen toiling in the rain and a gentleman—presumably the architect—desperately trying to get his orders followed but refusing to leave the sanctity of his carriage. Da had smiled when he saw four large sundials intended for each of the pillar's sides. He'd nodded towards the architect. "Must be an optimist," he'd said.

Receiving more use over the intervening years was the drinking fountain at its base, now a touch more worn than the rest of the structure as a result. The street split here, going down Bow Lane in one direction—towards the Royal Hospital and the road to Inchicore—and continuing in the other by the City Workhouse in the direction of Naas and the farms of Kildare. "Perfect," he said to Fergal. "Should catch them coming from both ways."

"We'll get all the people coming in off Echlin Lane from the canal too. Everyone else is fighting for scraps, but we could sew the whole thing up right here."

"Wouldn't be too much bother carting everything down here if we go by Rainsford Street and skip our friends back there at the gate." Jimmy rubbed his hands together. "This could work out nicely."

"You still thinking about America?"

Jimmy's eyes narrowed. "Who told you that?" He looked both ways, even though nobody was in earshot.

"You did, you fool." Fergal laughed. "When you were drunk the other night."

"Well, I shouldn't have. Ma doesn't know yet. So keep your trap shut." He locked eyes with Fergal.

"You haven't told Brigid?"

He paused, wondering how much he should share. "I want to *bring* her. She has no one to look after her if I take off."

"She has Nora."

"Nora has eight children, three grandchildren, and

two rooms for the lot of them. She'd have to put half of them in the Workhouse just to fit Ma's bed. And even if we could shove her in there somehow…" He shook his head. "With her weak lungs, it would kill her. She needs space to breathe." He sighed. "Which means I need to save enough for two tickets."

Fergal scratched his chin while Jimmy fretted. "Was talking to a fella there the other day who was on about some timber ship going from Limerick." He held his hands up. "Don't take this as Gospel now, I'm only repeating what I heard."

"Go on."

"There's this boat. It comes over from the colonies in Canada once or twice a year, loaded with timber, and has almost nothing to take back. The captain fills it any way he can."

"How much?"

"Varies."

"At a guess?"

"Don't hold me to this…"

"Jesus Christ, I won't, just tell me."

"Four pounds, is what I heard."

"Four? Are you sure?" asked Jimmy. "That's half price."

"According to your man, at least."

Jimmy rubbed his hands together. "Four pounds!"

"Now, don't get—"

"Ah, don't mind that." He clapped Fergal on the back and started striding towards St. James' Gate. "Come on, let's get home and grab our carts before someone else has the same idea." He started towards Thomas Street. "Four pounds? I could have that by Christmas, if I'm smart."

The Watch detained them for more than ten minutes of imbecilic questioning, despite Jimmy explaining he was a resident of Thomas Street. He turned to Fergal once they were eventually allowed to pass through. "*Definitely* going back the other way."

Twenty minutes later, Jimmy wheeled his cart up Thomas Court toward the top of Rainsford Street. Fergal was already at the corner, puffing away on a bowl of tobacco. Jimmy set his cart down to let Fergal finish his smoke. He was ranting about the new Fever Hospital on Cork Street again. Fergal had only two or three topics of conversation—all things that annoyed him in a trivial way, but which he constantly felt the need to remind himself of, as if they were players at the old Theatre Royal on Smock Alley and were destined to re-run the same unsuccessful show for all eternity. "It's the wrong place for it," he said for the umpteenth time. "I don't know why they didn't build it outside the city."

"I don't think they'll be wandering the streets, Fergal."

He exhaled towards Jimmy. "Let's see if you're this calm about it when you get the fever."

"Don't worry." He smiled. "If I get the fever, I know exactly what I'll do."

"What's that, then?" asked Fergal, tipping the spent tobacco to the ground.

Jimmy enveloped him in a big hug. "Run right over to Chamber Street and give you a sloppy wet kiss."

"Get off me!" Fergal shoved him away and picked up the handles of his cart. "Let's go make some coin." They continued down Rainsford Street until they reached the newly built harbor for the Grand Canal, already crowded with longshoremen, stevedores, and tax collectors, as well as a whole rake of porters flitting about the place like mayflies. Jimmy wondered how anyone kept track of it all.

They picked their way through the crowd and traversed the short stretch of Echlin Lane onto James' Street, where they were out of view of the Watch as long as they didn't stray too far from their patch. The pair began setting up right behind the drinking fountain at the fork in the road—a perfect spot with their backs to the side wall of a smart-looking grocery with an entrance on either street. *He must be doing well*, Jimmy figured, examining the structure. It looked like the rear of the building had previously been a dwelling, or perhaps a yard, but the proprietor had slowly expanded his concern. Fergal elbowed him in the ribs. The grocer was eyeing them up from inside his shop, looking none too happy.

"I'll deal with him," Jimmy said. "You finish here."

"We'll both go. Strength in numbers and all that."

He nodded. "Let me do the talking, though. You keep quiet until he names his price, and then immediately object."

"Ah, for fuck's sake, why do I always have to play the—"

"Perfect." Jimmy clapped him on the back. "Just the right amount of anger." He rapped on the window and beckoned the grocer outside. "Best to meet him on neutral ground," he said, over his shoulder.

The grocer was ruddy-faced, his balding pate offset by the most luxuriant sideburns, as if all the hair had migrated from his crown. "Now, boys," he said, his thumbs curling around the straps of his immaculate apron. "I don't know what you're up to here, but you may as well put a stop to it. When the Militia finds out, you'll be in all sorts of hot water."

Fergal leaned forward. "They better not find out then."

Jimmy glared at his friend for a moment before forcing a smile and returning his gaze to the grocer. He removed his cap. "Please excuse my associate, Mr.—" His eyes flicked to the sign. "Dunning. We are fellow tradesmen from The Glib Market."

"I don't care if you're from Jerusalem, this spot isn't designated for traders."

"We're well aware of that," said Jimmy, feeling the negotiation slipping away. "But I have a proposal for you."

The grocer paused just for a moment, and Jimmy continued before the man could get a word in. "This sorry business on Thomas Street has displaced us from our usual place of business, and we were hoping to set up here temporarily—"

"Five shillings," said Dunning.

Fergal was fit to explode, but Jimmy put an arm across his chest and locked eyes with the grocer. "I deal in hides, and my associate here is in the skin trade. We won't be taking any of your business."

"Four shillings."

"In fact," said Jimmy, "we'll add to it."

The grocer laughed. "How do you figure that?"

"Our customers like to take their time inspecting the merchandise. If they are seeking repast, we will insist they frequent your establishment rather than the *dangerous* alehouses on Thomas Street." Jimmy smiled.

"Three shillings," the grocer said with a nod. "Final offer."

Jimmy's smile turned to a grimace. "I'll be frank with you. At that rate, it's simply not worth our while. But I'll do you the honor of taking you at your word." He replaced the cap on his head. "Thank you for considering our proposal." He turned to Fergal. "We'll get a cheaper patch at the Ormond, but only if we hurry."

"You're the boss," grumbled Fergal, heading for the carts.

The grocer stepped forward to block their path. "Hang on now, boys. There's no need to be like that. I'm sure we can come to some kind of arrangement."

Jimmy ignored him and began packing up.

"Two shillings," said the grocer. When he got no response, he jostled Jimmy's elbow to catch his attention. "All right. A shilling, but that covers today only, and we'll see how it goes." Fergal and Jimmy shared a look.

"And you pay me now." Dunning added.

"I'll agree to a shilling if we can pay you at six, when we knock off."

Dunning laughed. "Not a chance. If the Militia comes and you boys scarper, I'll be left holding the bucket of piss." He fixed Jimmy with a stern look. "Half now," he insisted, "and half later."

Out of the corner of his eye, Jimmy saw Fergal give a small shake of his head. "May I confer with my associate?"

"By all means," said the grocer. "I'll be inside."

When he had left, Jimmy turned to Fergal. "Well?"

"I'm just wondering where you learned that flowery talk."

"Helps if one speaks their language," said Jimmy, raising his nose into the air and assuming a haughty demeanor. "But come hither, my boy. What do you think?"

"Doesn't matter what I think." Fergal's face scrunched up. "I don't have the money and neither do you."

Jimmy waved a hand. "Don't mind that. You think it's worth it? Or are we better off heading a bit further down the road."

Fergal peered down James' Street, and then down Bow Lane. "It's the perfect spot," he conceded.

"So we're agreed?"

"Except for the half-shilling."

"I'll handle it," said Jimmy. He rummaged through his bags until he found what he was looking for: a fancy riding crop that had been left with him on deposit for a bill that was ultimately never paid. He waved it at Fergal, smiling.

"Going to beat it out of him?"

"Something like that."

He pushed open the grocer's door, almost gasping at how clean and orderly the shop was. The long, thin grocery stretched all the way back to the other street and housed a staggering array of goods—moustache grease, cravat straighteners, pints of animal blood, and more prosaic items such as eggs, salted fish, and the greenest apples he'd ever seen.

"Stop right there," Dunning said, hurrying towards him. He jabbed a finger at Jimmy's boots. "Don't trail that muck in here, I'm only after sweeping the place."

Jimmy stared down at the neat black-and-red tiles his boots had desecrated. Mumbling an apology, he tried to gather himself and remember his speech. "My good man," he finally began. "We accept your offer."

The grocer eyed the riding crop, but Jimmy continued. "In lieu of the half-shilling, as all of our funds are tied up in the stock we'll be selling today, you may retain this fine piece of merchandise as security."

The grocer put up one fleshy hand, already protesting.

"I know, I know," Jimmy continued. "It's far too valuable. Custom-made, hand-stitched leather, a beautiful piece. Worth six shillings if it's worth a penny."

Dunning grabbed it out of Jimmy's hand and leaned in threateningly, his breath smelling of sour milk and cinnamon. "You better have paid by the time that bell tolls at six, in *cash*, or it'll be more than a lost riding crop you have to worry about."

Jimmy tried to smother his laughter as he backed out of the shop. "Let's get her set up," he shouted to Fergal.

The sun inched higher in the sky, casting dramatic shadows down James' Street. Jimmy plotted in the shadows while Fergal warmed himself in the sun's rays and nodded to the first farmers as they trickled in from the countryside, driving beasts ahead of them to the animal dealers at Haymarket or the butchers in Smithfield. They weren't the customers Jimmy was waiting for. He needed those traveling by foot. Men who had coin in their pockets and had traveled to Dublin for pleasure rather than business.

Soon enough, they came. From the farmlands out beyond Tallaght, lonely old men from Raheen and Ballinascorney and Knockbane, who wouldn't see another soul from one week to the next, greeted each other in Irish while washing their hands at the fountain. Inevitably, they wandered over to the two stalls. Most were just looking for news, or to share their own tales of woe, but they all wanted to know which rumors were true. Had Robert Emmet been captured? Did Thomas Russell escape to Paris? Was Miles Byrne returning with an army?

The Kildare farmers plagued the Wicklowmen about the rebel hero Michael Dwyer, demanding to know whether he'd really cheated death by posing as an itinerant beggar and walking right by the King's men. They were hungry for hope. Starving for it, even. But their Wicklow brothers forswore any real knowledge, even when pushed. Their eyes betrayed them, however, shining with obvious pride.

The Crown had tried everything to capture Dwyer, and the whole episode was a huge embarrassment to the Castle, especially since his fame had spread beyond the Glen of Imaal. He was held up as a hero by the whole country now, or those with rebel sympathies at least. An entire regiment of the famed Highland Guard couldn't pin him down. Crack Hessian mercenaries—hardened veterans of the American revolutionary wars, brought in specially to root him out—failed to corner their quarry.

And now the worst of the Militia had been let loose to terrorize the Wicklow Mountains. But no matter how many farmhouses they torched, or what price they put on Dwyer's head, they couldn't bring him in.

"If we had a Michael Dwyer in each county, we could tie up the whole British Army," suggested one Kildare native.

A proud farmer finally broke the code of silence. "Sure, if ye had the Wicklow Mountains in each county, they never would've taken over in the first place!"

The political talk, light-hearted as it was, made Jimmy nervous, but he nodded and smiled until the conversation took the usual, maudlin turn. Soon, whiskey was called for, and the grocer made busy. Trade was slow to begin with, but a crowd begets a bigger crowd, and within hours there were buyers among the talkers. Dunning got his shilling, and more besides, once those yapping farmers got the thirst. Ballad singers soon set up across the street, and urchins and flash girls worked the edges. Fergal fretted that their numbers would draw the attention of the Militia or the City Watch, but Jimmy assured him they would have more to worry about on Thomas Street.

By the end of the day, Jimmy was fit to drop.

"I'd say you did at least as well as me," Fergal said, a

gleam in his eye.

"Aye," said Jimmy. "Was a good day."

"Fancy heading to The Chop House? I could eat like a lord, and for once I can afford to."

He shook his head. "Ma will need her dinner."

"We can call on the way, bring her something."

"I can't. I need every penny for these tickets."

Fergal chewed his cheek for a moment. He snapped his fingers. "If I told you I was buying would it make any difference?"

Jimmy shook his head once more.

"Fair enough." Fergal admitted defeat. "Although I'm liable to get in fierce trouble on my own.

He smiled. "Watch out for Olocher."

BY THE TIME Jimmy got home and packed everything away in the small shed in the yard, he'd regained his spirits, helped along by the pleasant music of coins jangling in his pocket. Fergal hadn't given up on that drink so easily after all, and Jimmy had humored him. "Refuse nothing but blows," Da had always said. Jimmy had been able to get away before things got out of hand, but even so, he was a touch lightheaded. He'd eaten little more than a pie that was more grease and gristle than meat.

His tiredness grew with each step he took towards the garret he shared with Ma. The Riordans on the first floor were roaring and shouting, as usual. With twelve of them packed into the one room, he never could tell whether they were fighting or just trying to make themselves heard. It was hard to know over the noise of Biddy McGurk on the second floor, screaming at her husband again. It was all she seemed to do—even when he wasn't home. From what Jimmy knew of that shifty ragman, it was the least of what he deserved. Relative silence was a merciful relief when he finally got to the top floor. The din from below quieted to a manageable hum, and he could hear his own stomach growling as he entered the room. Dizzy from the drink, he bent to take off his breeches and then toppled backwards, coins spilling out across the floor in all directions.

Ma gasped and sat up in the bed. "Son, is that you?"

He stifled a chuckle. "Sorry, Ma."

"I thought it was the Militia." She blessed herself and then her eyes narrowed as she examined him. "You're drunk." Her nose wrinkled.

"Am not," he protested.

Ma's eyes widened again at the shillings strewn across

the floor. "Where'd you get all that, now?" She turned to Jimmy, her forehead creased in suspicion. "Were you out stealing?"

He sprang up from the floor. "I'm no thief."

"Then where'd you get all this money?"

His face flushed at the accusation, he began gathering the loose coins from the floor. "Never you mind."

"I do mind, James O'Flaherty, and I'll ask you again. Where did you get it?"

For a moment, he considered telling the truth, but something held him back. Once he started talking he wouldn't stop, and then it would all come out: his plans, Donal's secret message, the Limerick boat, America—the lot. And the next thing she'd be telling him to go on his own and to leave her die in peace. No, he couldn't have that conversation until everything was in place.

"I knew it." Ma took his silence as confession. She blessed herself and then turned her gaze up to the crucifix above the fireplace. "God save me, a thief for a son!" Her voice rose to a wail. "Have I not suffered enough?"

A thump on the wall answered her.

"Keep it down, Ma," hissed Jimmy. "I told you already: I'm no thief. I earned this fair and square. Promise."

She considered it for a moment, and held out one trembling palm. "Then give it to me."

"What?"

"Give it to me," she pressed, "and I'll keep it safe." When he hesitated, her voice grew soft, almost soothing. "I'll look after it for you."

"No." Jimmy shook his head. "You'll only give it to Nora or one of the children. This is for us." He puffed out his chest. "And I'll mind it."

She smiled. "You look just like your father right now, you know that? He was a proud man too. It was one of the things that first attracted me to him. That and his big, strong arms."

"Ma…"

"Keep your money, Jimmy."

He arched an eyebrow, unsure how to respond.

"I know why you want it anyway." She smiled in triumph and lay back on the pillow.

Jimmy approached the bed, feeling suddenly foolish in his smallclothes. "And why's that then?"

"Heard you were gallivanting again."

He tilted his head, but before he could respond, Ma continued. "A girl that pretty would need a good dowry."

He rolled his eyes. "I'm not getting married, Ma, and I don't have a girl."

"Whatever you say, son."

Thinking it best to leave it at that, he arranged his straw mattress on the floor beside her bed. "Goodnight, Ma."

He stretched out, staring at the cracked plasterwork on the ceiling, counting his takings over and over in his head, all the while worrying about his mother's rasping cough, which seemed a little worse again. If he could keep up this level of trade for the next couple of weeks while Thomas Street was closed off, he'd soon have more than enough for two tickets to America. Maybe he could even start thinking about a small plot of land somewhere.

Wouldn't that be something, he thought.

Land of my own. Our own, he corrected himself, imagining Ma sitting in the shade of the porch, gazing out over crop-filled fields. His eyelids grew heavier, and he slipped farther into the fantasy—mentally wiping the sweat from his brow as he approached the house, calling out as he stepped onto the mercifully cool porch.

Except it wasn't Ma greeting him with an ale.

It was Kitty.

3

JIMMY WOKE EARLY to a still-dark room and Ma snoring happily in the bed. He stumbled towards the chamber pot, bursting for a piss. Then, thinking better of waking Ma, he pulled on his breeches and grumbled his way downstairs, out the back door and into the yard to relieve himself in the alley behind the building. His grouchiness was not improved by emptying his bladder, and as he scratched his arms in the chill morning air, Jimmy remembered why. All night he'd tossed and turned, never once getting settled. He should have been happy, but he couldn't shake the feeling that something terrible was coming his way. *Then again,* he thought with a wry smile, *I always feel like shit in the morning.*

He trotted back upstairs to fetch the water bucket, and scrubbed himself in the yard before putting on his clean shirt and heading for Fergal's place on Chamber Street. The houses on that row were a little neater than the poorly maintained buildings of Thomas Street, and were populated mostly by weavers, who generally did a little better for themselves than the traders and tanners, or those working in the ever-expanding breweries and distilleries of The Liberties. The recent troubles didn't help; at such times, they all depended on each other. If the traders weren't earning, they couldn't drink, leading the publicans to reduce their orders and leaving the weavers with fewer brewer's wives to tempt with fine cloth. The thought made him anxious to get going, and he rapped on Fergal's door with a little too much force.

"Jesus Christ, Jimmy, I thought you were the Watch," Fergal's younger sister said. When she'd calmed down, Sinead explained that Fergal had never made it home last night. "I hope Olocher didn't get him," she said, her eyes bulging at the thought.

Jimmy almost laughed, although her fear was genuine. "Come on now, Sinead. Olocher isn't real. That's just a story people tell."

"Where's Fergal then?"

"Sleeping it off somewhere." The wail of a babe broke the morning silence, soon joined by two more. He grinned. "Somewhere quieter than here, I suspect."

Sinead allowed herself a slight smile.

"I have to go," Jimmy told her, pointing back up the street. "I want to get down there early. Fergal knows the spot."

"Would you not go and look for him, at least?"

"Sinead…"

"With everything that's been going on, he could be in the Castle." She gulped. "Or worse."

Jimmy stared down at the pavement, biting his tongue. Eventually, he met her gaze. "He could be anywhere."

She gripped his arm, digging her nails in. "But you know where he might be?"

He nodded.

"Thanks, Jimmy."

With the promise reluctantly pledged, Jimmy continued down The Coombe in the direction of St. Patrick's Cathedral. Despite his agitation, he couldn't help but smile at the charwomen as they left their homes almost in unison, like ducklings in search of their mother; the mystery of their timing was only solved when he spied the knocker-upper. Few working people here could afford a timepiece of their own, not one that could be relied upon. For a penny a month, Declan would add an address to his list, knocking to ensure the dwellers weren't late for work. Jimmy waved as he passed. And Declan tipped his cap, his other hand still gripping his pole, which was long enough to reach a first-floor window.

As he watched the charwomen scurrying off to work, Jimmy half-thought of heading back for his cart and leaving Fergal to find his own daft way home. But whenever he stopped to turn back, he pictured Sinead's eyes, wide with worry. Cursing himself, Jimmy picked up his pace and headed up Patrick's Street towards Christchurch, swearing he'd check one place and then get to work. *Fucking Olocher,* he thought. Men were sailing around the world, constructing buildings that could touch the sky, and creating vehicles powered by steam, yet people still believed in that stupid pig.

He had cheered somewhat by the time he reached Christchurch Cathedral, whistling as he walked down the Forty Steps into the den of whorehouses and drunkards known as Hell. A couple of whores thrust themselves forward to block his path, but their movements were lazy from the drink, and he brushed past them with ease. Jimmy quickened his pace, one eye on the brightening sky. When he reached Copper Alley, the brothel door was bolted shut. He was forced to hammer for some time before a peephole opened. "We're closed," a rasping voice said.

He leaned towards the peephole. "Is Fergal Hayes in there?" he asked. "Tell him Jimmy's waiting."

"You just missed him," replied the voice, before the peephole slid shut.

Jimmy didn't know whether it was a lie or not, but he'd fulfilled his promise to Sinead. Hurrying up Fishamble Street towards home, he felt guilty about not looking harder. But he could spend the whole day in Hell and barely scratch the surface. Besides, he'd only get grief off Ma if she heard where he had been, and he needed to get to James' Street before other traders from The Glib Market stole his patch.

Near Cornmarket House at the top of Thomas Street, he passed some poor unfortunate unconscious in the gutter, bloodied and soiled. A beggar boy sidled up and gave him a swift toe in the guts. When the prostrate drunkard didn't stir, the urchin rifled through his pockets, and then legged it.

"Olocher strikes again," said Jimmy with a chuckle.

The legend had taken root a few years back, and all sorts of stories now circulated about Olocher—the satanic pig that haunted The Liberties. He shook his head. The things people believed. If the Devil did exist, it was in the hearts of men—there was proof enough of that. Jimmy didn't see why anyone needed a possessed pig to make sense of the world. Although for some, it was just an excuse. Fellas would come into some money and decide to tear the arse out of it instead of salting it away or giving it to the wife for safekeeping. They'd go for one or two, and then, with the kind of logic you can only find in a whiskey bottle, they'd stumble down into Hell. There, the gambling houses, alehouses and brothels would soak up all the money and they'd often end up fighting someone—anyone—when the drink ran out. And when they finally made it home to hungry, worried spouses without two pennies to rub together—it was always Olocher who got them. Stranger still, the lads would believe it themselves by the time they were done with the telling.

Ma was still snoring when Jimmy got back home, so he set out some bread and milk on the sideboard and let her be. Normally, he was gone to work before the dairy opened, but Ma loved her milk and she'd welcome the surprise. He watched her sleep for a moment before slipping out the door.

Jimmy gathered his supplies and wheeled them up the long way again, avoiding the City Watch and already calculating his future profits. That greasy grocer would probably want an extra shilling today, but he could afford it now. Dunning must have done well out of the arrangement too, but he was sharp enough to guess how much he and Fergal had cleared. He'd kept poking his ruddy little head out of the shop to check, no matter how busy he got.

When he turned down Rainsford Street at the back gates of the always-busy Guinness Brewery, the sharp smell of burnt hops filled his nostrils. Jimmy nodded to a pair of coopers sharing a stout on the sly. This minor act of rebellion made him smile, and he whistled a jig as he followed the curving canal dock onto Echlin Lane. It was only once he turned onto James's Street that he stopped dead. A bustling crowd was already swarming around his spot. He dropped the handles of his cart and jogged over to Dunning, who was stood in the doorway of his shop, looking awfully pleased with himself.

"You're too late," he crowed.

Jimmy dug his fingers into his pocket. "How much did they give you? I'll better it."

"None of your concern." The grocer smiled all the more.

Jimmy ran his hands through his hair, desperately trying to think of a solution but already knowing he was beaten. "All right," he said. "It's my own fault anyway." He put his hand in his pocket once more. "But I'll pay you now for tomorrow. And there's more where that came from if you hold the spot for us."

Dunning ignored the proffered silver. Looking down his nose at Jimmy, he sniffed the air. "Price has gone up."

Before Jimmy could shuffle out more coin, the grocer continued, "And they've already paid for the week."

"The whole week?" Jimmy glanced back at his cart. A couple of young fellas were getting curious and fixing to have a rummage. He picked up a stone and fecked it at them. "Go on out of that."

The pair scattered, but as he turned back to Dunning he could see them in his peripheral vision, creeping back towards the cart. He spun and glared them into submission.

Ignoring the smirking grocer, Jimmy approached the traders who had usurped his position. "Rory," he called, recognizing one of the traders. "What's the deal here?"

"How are you, Jimmy?"

"None too fucking well. This is my spot. Me and Fergal found this yesterday."

Rory's smile hardened. "I'm sorry, Jimmy, but I've paid good money for this."

He bit back a response and went to rescue his cart from more prying locals. Scanning the area, he searched for a suitable patch, but the pathways were too narrow. That blasted drinking fountain, and the inevitable crowds around it, meant there was nowhere else to set up that wouldn't block the junction of the main road into Dublin, which would surely bring down the wrath of the

Militia; and that was unwise, especially without the appropriate trading licenses. No, he couldn't risk getting his stock seized.

Jimmy enviously eyed the herring sellers, wishing his operation were as mobile. If he could work the crowds as he pleased, like they did, not caring where he set up, he could make so much more. The ballad singers were even more flexible. Some might keep a little box to stand on, but all they really needed was a strong voice or just a good memory and a bit of passion. None of them had to worry about stock and licenses or customers and suppliers.

He leaned against his cart, watching a singer launch into a particularly lachrymose version of *Dunlavin Green*. Jimmy was embarrassed to feel his own eyes brimming with tears. When the ballad ended, he picked up the handles of his cart and began rolling his way back towards Rainsford Street.

It was still worth going the longer way home. Even if the Watch didn't delay him, or enquire about his licenses, he'd still have to get through the throng surrounding the gallows. Owen Kirwan was being hung today. With the larger crowds on a Saturday, he could be swamped by thieves as he picked his way through, and his trusty riding crop could only handle one light-fingered scamp at a time.

Up on Rainsford Street, the two coopers were still necking porter in the shade, and Jimmy shared a rueful smile with the pair. *Some people have it easy,* he thought. *Like Fergal. Not a care in the world.* Sure, Fergal had to hustle like the rest of them, and he had a large family he was expected to help support, but the responsibility never weighed on him. He was like a tinker's cat: you could throw him out a window and he'd still land on his feet. But then Fergal didn't have a sick mother and wasn't saving for passage to America. Jimmy was annoyed with himself for not cutting a deal with the grocer yesterday, but twice as angry that he'd wasted so much time hunting down his supposed friend, who was either still on the tear or hiding away with some hussy. Now he had another day at a loose end, with no money to be made.

He trudged home, swearing to wring Fergal's neck the next time he saw him. Olocher be damned.

JIMMY POSITIONED HIMSELF at the end of the counter, opposite the entrance. He didn't frequent the White Bull, but it was Fergal Hayes' local, so he was bound to show up at some point. His friend had some explaining to do.

Jimmy waited to catch the barman's eye; this wasn't the kind of place where you waltzed in and shouted your order—not if you weren't known. He took off his cap and placed it on the counter, silently cursing the lack of hooks under the bar. Running his hands through his unruly hair, he glanced up to the ceiling. It was far too low, as if the draughtsman had left off a foot and the builders never noticed. The floor was so old and warped that exposed nails stuck through everywhere. The regulars, he noticed, had developed a bandy-legged gait to avoid the worst of them, which had the unfortunate effect of making them look like they'd just ridden into town.

The White Bull got busier, and Jimmy finally got his drink. He sipped it, taking in the place. Even though it had always been a popular spot, he was surprised to see it so full. It had been firmly outed as a United pub after the failed Rising in July, but the same heads seemed to be here.

He accepted another pint from the barman, dipping his little finger in the stout's creamy head. This was his favorite part. The first blush, when anything was still possible. He smiled and took a gulp. Putting his pint back on the counter, Jimmy listened to the drinkers beside him talking about America. He wanted to scream, or throttle Fergal, but instead he took another sup and tried to relax. After a moment, he glanced around, curious as to their conversation but eager not to draw too much attention to himself; this was known as a United pub for a reason.

A fella called Mahaffy was leading the conversation; the others seemed to defer to him, at least. Jimmy knew him a little—knew of him, to be more accurate. Ma was always warning Jimmy that he was a troublemaker and to stay away. He could see why she'd formed that impression. Mahaffy had the maddest-looking eyes, which bulged right out of his head when he emphasized a point—and from where Jimmy was standing, just down the bar counter, that happened often enough.

He also had a habit of slowly raising his hand as he was outlining an argument, and then bringing it crashing down on the bar for the denouement. Jimmy watched with amusement as those near Mahaffy gripped their own drinks whenever his speech became more impassioned, lifting them a touch from the counter before he slammed down his fist, almost like clockwork. As the porter began to hit its mark, Jimmy imagined invisible twine connecting each drinker to the other, the barman winding up the whole contraption with each pull of the taps. He chuckled to himself until a couple of heads turned his way, upon which he pulled his cap down over his eyes and focused on the door, willing Fergal's arrival.

Soon enough, the conversation turned to the fate of the captured rebel leader, Robert Emmet. He'd evaded the authorities the night of his uprising a couple of months back. And for several weeks afterwards, competing rumors had circulated as to his plans and whereabouts. The Militia had even subjected his housekeeper, Anne Devlin, to a half-hanging.

'Half-hanging' was quite the euphemism, Jimmy thought. Those who suffered through one got all the pain from being strangled, but none of the relief from death. Survivors all told the same story. Usually, a rope was strung up over a tree branch in a rough fashion. When the victim started drifting, the soldiers let go of the rope, letting the victim's body plummet to the ground, only to be quickly hoisted aloft to begin choking anew. And all the while, they were questioned.

Anne Devlin didn't talk, but the Castle kept raising the bounty on Emmet's head until somebody cracked. The housekeeper's reward for her loyalty was a prison cell. *Another victim of this madness*, Jimmy thought, suddenly angry at all those around him. He tried to keep his temper in check as that old crone John Spenser, the local apothecary, challenged Mahaffy when he complained about the delay in Robert Emmet's trial. "I don't know," Spenser said. "This could be good."

"How so?" asked Mahaffy, his eyes already bulging.

Spenser spread his hands before him on the bar. "Well, if they need someone to turn King's Evidence, it means their case isn't too strong."

"It doesn't need to be!" Mahaffy laughed. "The verdict will have been decided long before he enters that courtroom. You can be sure of that."

"Then why delay?"

"To flush out the rest of them." Mahaffy lowered his voice. "You well know that Wicklow was ready to rise— they say Dwyer was at the edge of the city with his band, waiting for a signal—Kildare and Wexford too. Emmet is one of their own, remember."

"Aye, you're right there. I don't know why he didn't leave Ireland when he had the chance. Miles Byrne had more sense."

"It's a testament to the man. He was probably trying to make his way down to Dwyer, hole up there in the Wicklow Mountains and wait for the French."

"Lord save us," Jimmy groused to himself, realizing, when both men turned in his direction, that he'd still been too loud.

"What's that supposed to mean?" asked Mahaffy.

"Nothing," said Jimmy, shaking his head and already regretting his interjection. "Don't mind me."

But Mahaffy wasn't leaving it alone. "I know your type."

"Then you should know I'm the type who tends to his own affairs." Jimmy met his stare. "I'd appreciate it if you did the same."

"Fellas, fellas," the barman cautioned, seeing them square up to each other. "Take it handy, or take it outside."

"Thanks," said Jimmy.

"Don't be getting smart." The barman jabbed a finger at him. "If you want to mind your own business, don't butt in to their bloody conversation."

He raised his glass to the barman before draining its contents. "I'll be on my way, so." He made for the door, but a single word stopped him in his tracks.

"Coward."

Jimmy paused. The taunting behind him continued.

"Either that or a Castle spy."

He could feel the room's eyes on him as he turned. "I'm no traitor," he said.

"You're no patriot," Mahaffy sneered.

A hundred things he wanted to say crowded his brain, but he just shook his head and continued toward the door.

"Unlike your father."

"My father was a fool!" The crowd gasped as Jimmy glowered back over his shoulder. "Just like all of ye. What is this madness? How many have to die before you lot see sense? 'Wait for the French.' Are ye soft in the head, or what?"

The barman stepped out from behind the counter, balling his fists. "Was Napper Tandy stupid? What about Wolfe Tone or Lord Fitzgerald, were they stupid too? They died for Ireland."

"Died for Ireland!" Jimmy laughed. "The graveyards are overflowing with men who died for Ireland. And what the fuck did that ever achieve?"

He was answered with a punch.

4

J IMMY WINCED AS Ma finished treating his swollen eye. It was good to see her out of bed, even if it had required getting the lard beaten out of him. He hadn't heard her cough once this morning either. "How's it looking?"

"Would've been a lot better if you'd let me do this last night," she scolded him.

He focused on the dirty boot marks he'd left on her bedsheet when he'd collapsed at her feet. "Sorry for taking your *leaba* last night, I don't remember…" He trailed off as he stood, his chest aching.

"You're lucky you didn't get your ribs broken." Ma tutted. "Booting you on the ground, they were. I don't know what you said to them." She lifted his shirt to re-examine the bruising. "Or what you were doing down in The White Bull in the first place. Trouble, that crew." She waited for a response that didn't come. "Sit back down," she said, taking a bottle of amber liquid from the shelf.

"I'm all right for whiskey, Ma."

"It's not for drinking." She frowned at him. "Now be quiet while I remember this." Jar after jar came down from the shelf, some covered with so much dust that they mustn't have been opened for donkey's years. She sometimes squinted to read a faded label, other times sniffed the contents, but still she replaced each jar, unsatisfied. "Where is the bloody thing?"

"Where's what?"

"Quiet, you." She stared up at the ceiling for a minute, mumbling to herself, and then clicked her fingers. Ma grabbed a tin from the shelf and shoved her hand inside, drawing out a dusty little bottle made from dark glass. She smiled. "*Glasluibh chruinn*—wintergreen herb," she explained. "I haven't seen this in some time."

Her eyes seemed to fill with sadness. Jimmy opened his mouth to ask if she was all right, but then shut it again.

"We need to dilute it a little," she continued, decanting a couple of inches of whiskey into a smaller vessel, weakening it somewhat with water, and then adding several drops from the dark, mysterious little bottle. Jimmy watched with mounting curiosity.

"It's an old recipe," Ma said eventually, pinning him with a look he couldn't quite decipher. "Came in handy during your father's fighting days."

Jimmy raised an eyebrow. "I can't imagine Da losing his temper. No one could ever get a rise out of him, no matter how hard they tried."

"It was before you were born," she said, stirring the mixture. "Used to be terrible fighting around here—almost every Sunday at one point."

"The Liberty Boys?"

Ma smiled momentarily at the memory. "I think your father just wanted to fit in. We were only up from the country at that point, and he was looking for work. You know what the people around here are like. They look after their own. Everyone else can take a running jump."

"Was this before he had the stall?"

She waved a hand. "Well before that. He was getting bits of work laboring—one week at the distillery, the next at the brewery—nothing regular." She smiled. "He thought it would be a bit of a lark. 'City boys playing at Whiteboys,' was what he said. But when those fellas from The Ormond Market arrived with their big butcher's knives…"

"I thought that was all talk."

"You'd be surprised how many of those stories are true." Ma laughed. "Your poor Da was terrified. All the other lads with him pulled out knives and hooks and knuckledusters and axes. They must've thought he was mad, standing there with nothing more than his two fists."

Jimmy laughed along with her, and then clutched his chest in agony.

She set down the mixture and approached him, eyebrows drawn together. "Are you sure you haven't broken anything?"

Jimmy lifted up his shirt and traced the outline of his ribcage with the pads of his fingers—tenderly at first, then a little more firmly, wincing all the while. "Just bruised, I think."

"Your Da came home black-and-blue," she continued, "so I dug out this old recipe."

Jimmy leaned forward to sniff the open bottle. "What is it? Smells like it would rip your insides apart."

"A bad bottle," she said. "Used to sell them out the back door of Powers, before the bosses put a stop to it. But you can't drink it."

He scrunched up his nose.

"Well, you *can* drink it, but you'll be sick as a dog. Of course," she said, grabbing the bottle and putting it back on the shelf, "that wouldn't stop some." Ma nodded to the mixture. "Give that a few minutes to settle." She sat on the edge of her bed and fixed him with a serious look. "So you may as well talk. Who did this to you?"

Jimmy knew there was no point arguing with her. She'd probably heard half the story already, so it would be better if the other half came from his mouth. He took a deep breath and then explained how the argument started, omitting his own comments that had triggered the row, and that he'd managed to get a few digs in himself.

By the time he was done, his mother was stony faced. "Be careful of that fella Mahaffy."

"I know—"

"Don't give me any of your 'I know, Ma.'" Her voice sharpened. "He's nothing but trouble. Keep out of his way."

"He said he was a friend of Da's."

She stood suddenly, her face reddened. "Well, he's no friend of mine!"

Her fury surprised Jimmy.

"Where did your father's friends leave him? Bleeding out in a ditch, like an animal. Buried in some hole on Vinegar Hill with a bunch of strangers. I can't even visit his grave. My own husband! It breaks my heart. Friend," she harrumphed. "All the more reason to avoid him."

She stirred the mixture vigorously before turning on Jimmy and jabbing the spoon in his direction. "That was your father's problem," she said. "He wanted everyone to like him."

"Ma—"

"I know I shouldn't speak ill of the dead." She blessed herself. "And may God forgive me for what I'm about to say, for your father was a kind man and a faithful husband, but he was too nice sometimes. Gave people too much credit. They'd take advantage of him— in little ways, for the most part, but it boiled my blood to see it, knowing how hard he worked to put food on the table."

Jimmy instinctively peered towards the mantelpiece, his jaw clenched. Those long-sold books had only graced the house because his father was a soft touch. The fancy booksellers on Parliament Street could trade off their reputation and pawn off a couple of books if they felt like avoiding a debt. He'd had an inkling of that as a child, while his father taught him the letters and struggled not to yawn.

Da used to say that he'd promised God he would teach all his children how to read and write, and the big fella upstairs did his part by giving him only one. Other times, when he was drunk and happy and holding little

Jimmy aloft, he'd claim that his son was so perfect God must have decided to close the factory out of fairness to all the other families. Jimmy had been too young, back then, to understand Ma's forlorn expression.

He watched as Ma dribbled a small amount of the mixture onto one fingertip, rubbed it into the back of her hand, and then stoppered the bottle with a small cork. She gave the bottle another quick shake and set it back down on the table. "Still needs to settle more."

Jimmy eyed the fluid inside with skepticism.

"It's a salve," Ma explained. "Should reduce the pain of those nasty bruises." She quirked one eyebrow. "Won't do much for your brains, though, so you'll have to get a little more cute with these fellas all on your own. Can you manage that?"

He met her eyes and nodded, noticing she was blinking back tears. Ma turned away to fuss over the bedsheets, balling them up before placing them near the door.

When he said nothing, she finally turned to him—a bittersweet expression on her face. "He was clever in other ways, to be fair." She uncorked the bottle and dripped a little of the liquid onto her hands again. "Take off that shirt now, son."

He fumbled with the buttons, wincing as Ma rubbed

the warm salve into his chest in a gentle, circular motion until she'd covered the area from his sternum to his belly button.

"Turn around," she commanded. "Your father had enough sense not to go along the next time. Well," she corrected herself, "he went, but not to fight."

Jimmy enjoyed the glow spreading through his muscles, the tingling of the salve before the area numbed altogether. He took a deep breath to test his ribs, but this time he felt nothing. The pain was gone. He swiveled around. "What do you mean, 'he went, but not to fight'?"

Ma waved the half-full bottle. "I hadn't done this in years, so I ended up making far more than we needed. Your father took the rest around to the lads, trying to get into their good graces, I suppose. Somewhere along the way, he got the bright idea of selling it at the next fight." She laughed. "He figured there'd be plenty of takers."

Jimmy grabbed the bottle, staring hard into its contents.

"Did all right out of it too," his mother added, but Jimmy was barely listening. His mind was whirring.

"Why didn't you make more?" he asked.

"Ah," she waved a hand. "I think that was when he got the job in the Anchor Brewery. Regular money.

Safer. Besides, they put a stop to all that fighting soon after."

"But someone *could* make money out if it."

Ma thought for a moment, then nodded. "If you can get cheap spirits. That's the bit that'll cost you. But any strong drink will do." She took the bottle from him and poured some more out into her palm, rubbing her hands together. "Now let me put some more on your back."

Jimmy turned to the wall, already plotting a new route to America.

AT THE TOP end of Thomas Street, just before the junction with Francis Street, Jimmy surveyed his temporary new patch. It was in the shadow of the Cornmarket House building, which straddled the street and forced the traffic either side. Mulligan's was opposite, a rowdy spot, but one that served the best stout in the area. The large structure housing Powers was right next-door, one of many thriving whiskey distilleries in The Liberties now. But it wasn't his old spot. It wasn't The Glib. His regular customers travelling up to Dublin this morning from the south might not be able to find him. He sighed, reminding himself he had to make the best of it. The scaffold still stood at St. Catherine's Church. It wasn't quite finished its grim duty, and the Castle had ordered it to be left up, no doubt encouraging news of the grisly executions to make its way down the country.

Today, there were to be two hangings, both taking place up at Misery Hill. The Castle knew Thomas Street would be swamped with farmers, from the time Mass finished until the crowds traveled home in the evening. News of the street's closure may not have made it as far as Kildare or Wexford, so, fearing disorder, they moved today's executions to a quieter spot, over past Trinity College, allowing the hide traders to temporarily set up here at the opposite end of Thomas Street.

Jimmy's bruised face received a few queer looks as he wheeled his cart up to the designated spot, but his accompanying scowl kept comments to a minimum. Paulie Grogan was leering at him, clearly itching to say something, but at least Fergal had enough sense to stay out of his way. In truth, the scowl was more about deflecting their enquiries than any sour mood. Jimmy was more nervous than anything. A ripple of excitement at how they'd go today knocked the frown off his face. They'd had only enough alcohol to make five bottles of the tincture, but that would give him a chance to test the reaction. If it was a success, he could invest in more—maybe even get some help and start selling it to the grocers.

The road slanted downhill a little, so Jimmy bent to secure his cart with a couple of loose cobbles. When he straightened up, Paulie Grogan was there, examining one of Ma's bottles. "What's this?" he asked. "Porter?"

"Never you mind." Jimmy snatched the bottle and put it back with the rest at the front of his display, arranging his remaining stock so it wasn't taking up much space, a job made easier by his dwindling supplies. He didn't dare invest in more leather until he got through the next few weeks.

"Suit yourself." Paulie deliberately bumped the table with his hip, upending one of the bottles. Jimmy caught it just before it rolled off the side.

He met the trader's mocking stare. "Watch it," he growled.

"Or what?" Paulie pointed at Jimmy's face and smirked. "You going to beat me up?"

"Lads," cautioned another trader, shoving them apart. "Let's try to avoid a fistfight before the first customer arrives." He eyed each of them in turn. "There'll be plenty of time for that nonsense when we're done making money. Remember, we have to keep our noses clean today."

Jimmy eyeballed Paulie, but resumed his position behind the table and turned his attention to his first customer: a squat old fella with his pants hitched so far up his chest it looked as if his torso had been shrunk by a witch.

"Is that some kind of porter?" the old man asked, licking his lips.

"No," replied Jimmy, struggling to keep the edge from his tone. "It's medicine."

"I'd say it is, all right."

"Like an ointment, I mean. You rub it onto bruises or sore muscles. Helps with the pain."

The old man looked skeptical. "Sure, what good is that to me?" He curled a finger and pressed it against his heart. "All my pain's right here. Ten years it is since my Maura left me. Ten long, long, lonely years." He set the bottle back down. "You know what does help with pains of the heart?"

"I don't know," Jimmy said, gritting his teeth.

The old man smiled. "Porter!" He scooted off across the street, in the direction of Mulligan's pub.

The day passed in the same manner—his only customers were people wanting nothing more than a quick chat before heading about their business, or into

Mulligan's. His pitch improved somewhat, but he never came close to a sale.

Until Kitty Doyle appeared.

A FEW HOURS earlier, just after the bells at St. Catherine's had announced the arrival of noon, Kitty knocked on the side-door of The White Bull and was led into the private room at the back, where Mahaffy was already ensconced. He greeted her with a wolfish grin, shoving his half-finished plate of cabbage and ham to one side and wiping his mouth with the back of his hand. "The rat has outlived his usefulness." He fixed Kitty with a stare as she sat opposite. "It's all set for Friday."

She avoided his eyes, focusing on the table. "Are you sure this time? I don't want—"

"We're sure. This Friday." He paused. "Can we depend on you?"

"Of course," she answered without hesitation.

Mahaffy continued to eyeball her. "Good," he said, finally. "I always knew we could."

Kitty met his glare for a moment before staring up at the ceiling and exhaling. Her eyes traced the cracked plasterwork as she waited for her heart to calm. Once she was confident her voice would remain firm, she returned her gaze to Mahaffy. "Anything else?"

He reached across the table, as if to comfort her, but Kitty withdrew her hand. A sad expression passed over his face momentarily, but then his eyes hardened. "There is one more matter." He pursed his lips. "The O'Flaherty boy. What have you been able to find out?"

"I don't think he's our man."

"Are you sure?"

"Well... he's penniless, for one."

"Come on now." Mahaffy laughed. "A lot of fellas put on the poor mouth, especially if they've been taking money from the Castle."

"I'm no fool. This is different. He's desperate for money, but—"

"Why?"

"His mother is sick, and he wants to bring her to America. He's been trying to make money for the tickets, but he's just scraping by."

He considered this for a moment. "There's something about him I don't trust."

"Aside from the shiner he gave you?"

Mahaffy instinctively reached for his swollen eye before catching himself. "I want you to get closer to him."

"But why?"

"Jesus Christ, Kitty. Do I have to spell it out to you?"

"I don't like it," she said after some time.

Mahaffy met her burning stare with one equally as fierce. "You don't have to."

Kitty nodded her assent and then made her way out the side door. As she slipped into the crowds on Thomas Street, augmented by the devout pouring out of all the little Catholic churches hidden down alleys and laneways, she pondered the failed Rising and the talk that the British had infiltrated every aspect of their operation. She was starting to wonder whether the authorities really did know everything in advance, whether they were so confident in their ability to nullify the threat that they didn't even bother rounding up the leaders before the rebellion started. That they *let it happen*.

The United Irishmen were still piecing it all together—not helped by half their leadership being behind bars or in exile. But it was certainly true that someone had been spreading false rumors on the morning in question. Crucial reinforcements from Kildare and Wicklow were turned back on the Dublin Road. The Belfast crews had all been told to stand down. Castle spies seemed everywhere, at every key point, spreading the message that the uprising had been postponed.

Rather than some quixotic endeavor or a drunken riot—as it had been portrayed in the press—Robert Emmet and the United Irishmen had an intricate plan to grab the seat of British power in Ireland: Dublin Castle itself. All the barracks surrounding the city were to be occupied first, preventing the Army from reinforcing the Castle. The rest of the country was ready to rise the following day—once the Castle was seized, paralyzing any British response—but instead Emmet was left with just 300 men caught up in a brawl on Thomas Street, quickly corralled by troops that poured from the uncaptured barracks.

Emmet's men weren't even properly armed. The supposedly loyal man sent to collect the guns had absconded with the money. Then there was the 'accident' at the Bridgefoot Street depot, which meant the Rising had to be moved forward several months—well before the planned arrival of the French invasion fleet. All of that might have seemed like bad luck, but once the trials commenced, it seemed the Castle had been watching for some time. The extent of their infiltration was shocking, helped on by the huge amounts of coin being spread around to reward anyone with half a scrap of information on rebel activity.

Kitty carefully examined the faces of the men she

passed. Most looked desperate enough to accept the King's shilling. Any of them could be informants. Sure, it looked like they'd been played by the British right from the start. Mahaffy was right. The spies had to be rooted out. There could be no repeat of the mistakes of July. Robert Emmet's fatal flaw had been showing mercy when he should have been ruthless. This time, the turncoats would pay for their treachery. All of them.

She stopped under the awning of Mulligan's, watching Jimmy from across the street as he bickered with Paulie Grogan—a known spy, who would be dealt with once they were finished feeding him false information. Could Mahaffy's suspicions be correct? She still wasn't sure about Jimmy. He was a suspicious sort, and she had to play this one carefully.

Kitty smoothed her hair. Time to play the sensitive maiden again.

SHE DIDN'T MEET his eyes at first, instead inspecting his merchandise slowly and deliberately, but without, he noticed, any kind of expert eye. She just picked each item up for a moment before casting it aside. Jimmy was anxious to get the exchange over with, feeling more uncomfortable with each passing moment and increasingly conscious of his bruised face. He cleared his throat. "Can I help you with something?"

She didn't even look up at that; a brief headshake was her only response. He was about to press her further when an elderly man with a shock of white hair and a thin moustache shuffled to the table and eyed the dark fluid in one bottle. "Is that porter?" he asked, stooped over his cane.

Jimmy gritted his teeth. "If it's porter you're after, you'd best head over to Mulligan's." The old fella tipped his hat and ambled in the direction of the pub, prodding each cobblestone in his path as if he feared it wouldn't hold his slight frame.

"Some salesman you are."

He looked up to see Kitty Doyle's striking green eyes twinkling with mischief.

"Never you mind," he replied, feigning indifference.

"What is it anyway?"

Jimmy sighed. "It's a potion for—"

"Like a witch's potion? Will it turn me into a bat?"

"If only," he murmured. Jimmy cleared his throat again. "It's a salve—an ointment of sorts. For cuts and sores. Bruises, bad joints."

"You're still not really selling it to me."

He flushed. "And what would you know about it?"

Without answering, Kitty grabbed a bottle and ran towards the old man who was still shuffling towards Mulligan's at a snail's pace. Jimmy watched with a mixture of shock and amazement as Kitty convinced the old codger to hitch up his shirt, right there in the street. She began massaging the tincture into his upper hip, ignoring the reproving stares of the women and the catcalls of the men. After she'd finished, she held out her hand. The now-smiling old man dropped some coin into her palm in exchange for the rest of the bottle, and skipped across to Mulligan's, beaming from ear to ear.

Kitty approached the stall with a triumphant smile on her face and threw the money down in front of him. "What have you to say now?" she challenged, raising her voice above the jeers of the other traders.

"You're short." He fingered the coins. "It's eight pence a bottle, not six."

Her nostrils flared. "You're a prick, Jimmy O'Flaherty, you know that?" she spat, and then stormed off in the direction of St. Catherine's.

"I think she likes you." One of the traders gave him a friendly punch on the arm. "You must tell us your secret."

He glared in response and pocketed the change,

fussing over his display. Despite his regular glances down Thomas Street, Kitty had melted into the crowd. Not wanting to show his hand, Jimmy distracted himself with the chatter coming from the neighboring stall. It was a familiar topic. All the talk on Thomas Street today was of the rebel leader's housekeeper, Anne Devlin—a Wicklow girl now imprisoned in Dublin Castle. Rumor was she had been tortured to force Robert Emmet to confess. Any mercy the authorities might have been expected to show a woman in such circumstances was abandoned once they discovered she was a cousin of Michael Dwyer, the rebel still holding out in the Wicklow Mountains and still thumbing his nose at the Crown, five years on from the '98 Rebellion.

"You the fella with the magic potion?" A wiry codger with scrawny arms but an impressive paunch stood before him. "Billy Mahon said his hip never felt better." He picked up the bottle. "Is this the stuff?"

"Aye," said Jimmy, as the fella counted out six coins. "Actually, the price is… never mind. Sixpence will do." The old man thanked him and made for Mulligan's. Jimmy did some quick calculations. Sixpence a bottle would cover his costs, but it would wipe out most of his profits. However, if each old fella told two more, he could be in business. "Tell all your friends," he shouted after him.

One of the nearby traders eyed him coldly.

"What?" Jimmy said, then he remembered shouting at Kitty. "Oh. Sorry. I'll make it right."

"You should," the man said, approaching the stall. "I wasn't codding earlier. I think she's keen on you."

Jimmy's face must have betrayed his surprise, because the man went on.

"I'm serious," the trader insisted. "Sure she was asking me and Paulie all about you the other day. Swore us to secrecy and all."

Jimmy fought to keep himself from smiling, forgetting his bruised face.

5

ON MONDAY EVENING, when he was finished work for the day and tiredness had sunk deep in his bones, Jimmy rolled his cart beyond the front door of his building and down toward the silent gallows in front of St. Catherine's. A solitary candle, burnt almost down to its nub, still flickered on the stage; whether it was in tribute to those already executed, or in thanks that no one had been hung today, Jimmy wasn't sure. He set his cart down and walked over, drawn to its sputtering flame.

Jimmy cupped his hands around the waning candle, and its flame wavered for a moment before coming back to life. He stepped back, leaning against his cart, staring up towards the scaffold. It was shorn of its rope but otherwise intact. He was surprised no one had burned the whole thing down over the weekend.

"I think they leave it up there to taunt us."

He hadn't even noticed Kitty approach. Jimmy

glanced briefly at her face before returning his gaze to the flickering flame.

"I'm sorry about yesterday," she continued.

He wheeled around. "I'm the one who should apologize."

"I should have asked the price."

Jimmy watched her stare at the gallows. "You know how to sell, that's for sure," he said after a minute. "Some show you put on yesterday."

Kitty flushed with embarrassment before changing the subject. She gestured at the scaffolding. "Who is it tomorrow?"

"We don't know yet. There's another trial still going on over in Green Street, but the fella from earlier—Walter Clare—was respited."

"Respited?"

"I don't know what it means either. I think they're still holding him. He was found guilty, but they didn't announce the sentence. That's all the broadsheet said."

Kitty's eyes narrowed. "Did you know him?"

"Sorry." Jimmy shook his head. He watched as she struggled with her emotions, her eyes fixed on the gallows. It was a tricky subject to broach, but he had to know. He considered the right words for a moment. Using as soft a tone as he could muster, he said, "Is there… a particular name you want me to keep an ear out for?"

"All of them." She turned to face him, counting the dead on her fingers as she named them. "Edward Kearney, Thomas Maxwell Roach, Owen Kirwan, James Byrne." She dropped her eyes. "Someone has to remember."

His mother had said the same after the executions didn't even make the papers, despite her antipathy towards the rebels. Kitty's eyes welled up, and a tear escaped down her cheek.

It took all Jimmy's restraint to stop himself brushing it away.

She turned to his cart laden with bottles of Ma's concoction. "More of your witch's brew?"

Jimmy laughed. "Was up all night with Ma making more, running around looking for bottles. We sold out yesterday… thanks to you."

"You're back in business then."

"Not if I can't shift this lot. Today was very slow, but it's only Monday, so we'll see."

Kitty's face grew serious. "If you need any help, I could do with the coin."

He was taken aback. "Well, I don't know." Kitty didn't make any attempt to hide her disappointment.

"You were very good," he said. "It's just that—"

"Forget it."

Jimmy cursed as he watched her walk away. "I can't pay very much."

She stopped.

"But perhaps we can come to some kind of arrangement."

Kitty turned to face him, her lips drawn tight. "What does that mean, exactly?"

"Commission." He ran some quick numbers in his head. "I'll pay you a penny for each bottle you sell. And we'll see how it goes for a few days. How does that sound?"

"It sounds good." She smiled, waving goodbye and walking hastily in the direction of Cutpurse Lane. After she had disappeared into the crowd, Jimmy picked up the handles of his cart and began wheeling it towards home. A voice stopped him in his tracks.

"Be careful of her." He wheeled around to see a sheepish looking Fergal Hayes holding his hands up. "Before you say anything," he said, "let me apologize."

Jimmy bit back a sharp response and just nodded for him to continue instead.

"I heard what happened in The White Bull," Fergal continued, "and I'm sorry. It's my fault. I suppose you were in there looking for me, and I fucked up that morning."

Jimmy raised his chin, eyeing him with obvious suspicion. "I don't understand what you mean."

"I made a balls of it," he said. "What more can I say? You know how it goes. One thing led to another that night and I didn't make it back home until noon the next day."

"No," Jimmy said, his tone harsher now. "I'm talking about Kitty. What do you mean 'be careful'?"

"Just a friendly warning, is all."

"What's that supposed to mean?" He balled his fists.

"Don't get thick with me, Jimmy, I'm trying to help."

He exhaled through his nose, trying to calm himself. "Cryptic warnings don't help me."

"Just be careful." Fergal looked like he was going to say something else but he stopped himself. "That's all I'm saying," he said, eventually.

"But you haven't explained why you're saying it!"

Fergal looked down at his hands.

"I understand now." Jimmy laughed. "You're jealous."

"What?"

"You're jealous. I can see it now. You're always boasting about your prowess with the women. Lording it over me. And when someone shows interest in me, for once, you warn me away."

"Jimmy—"

"I've heard enough." He picked up the handles of his cart and wheeled it towards home. Only later on, as he was packing away his stock, did he understand Fergal's expression. He wasn't jealous or bitter or angry; he was afraid.

KITTY TURNED OUT to be a natural. Her easy way with customers made them feel as if *she* were the one doing the favor by selling them something. But the really surprising part was the type of customers stopping by: men who normally wouldn't give Jimmy the time of day, mostly due to the slights, real or imagined, that an Irishman routinely accumulates. Kitty could chat to anyone about anything. Although he noticed that when the talk turned to family, she would change the subject. Not that there was anything particularly unusual about that—it was a topic he was circumspect on himself—but it did make him wonder whether she'd also lost someone in '98. It would explain her reaction to the executions, he figured.

He pondered that while watching her make one sale after another. She was proving so successful that Jimmy calculated he'd need more stock in a day or two, certainly before the weekend. As the day progressed, he began to notice some signs of affection from her: blushing when he complimented her on a sale, leaving a hand on his back for just a moment, and, sometimes, gazing into his eyes with a look he swore was longing. He saw Fergal watching too, his scowl only confirming yesterday's suspicions.

Things were going so well that Jimmy decided to ask her for a drink when they knocked off. He wondered if that would be inappropriate, what with Kitty working for him, and then struggled with whether she'd feel uncomfortable or compelled to humor him. It troubled him for a whole hour until he realized he could frame it as a celebratory drink between colleagues—marking a good first day and the launch of a new partnership. *Yes,* he thought, *that could work.* Any awkwardness would be minimized if she refused, and they could go their separate ways. It seemed the perfect plan, until just after the four o'clock bells when news came through that Felix Rourke had been sentenced to death.

Noticing that Kitty was close to tears, he asked if she wanted to take a few minutes to compose herself. She scurried off down Thomas Street without another word. When she returned, it was clear she'd been crying, although her expression was stony. She continued to work, but she was just going through the motions. By five, with the street quiet, he told her to knock off early. Kitty nodded her thanks and left without even asking for her pay.

It put Jimmy in a glum mood all the way home. He packed his stock away in the shed, covered his cart with the tattered old bedsheet, and then climbed the stairs, hoping his mother wouldn't mind what he'd brought home for dinner. Mackerel had never been her favorite, but it was half-price. He pushed the unlocked door open again, and was about to reprimand Ma for the umpteenth time when he saw her on the floor beside the chamber pot, unconscious.

"Ma!" He slid down onto the floor, rolling his mother onto her back. Still breathing. "Wait here. Don't move." He flew down the stairs onto the street, grabbed the first person he recognized, and sent them running for the doctor. Then he raced all the way back to the top floor and burst through the door.

"Jimmy…"

Ma was on her side now.

He knelt down, cradling her head as gently as he

could. "Jesus, Ma, what happened?"

She was groggy and took a moment to respond.

He noticed her forehead was roasting.

"I'm grand," she said eventually, her voice as weak as her appearance. She struggled to sit upright.

"Slowly now," warned Jimmy, supporting her back. A brutal cough rose from her chest, a sawing hack that doubled her over. Her body shuddered as the fit finally eased.

"Do you want me to move you over to the bed?"

Ma shook her head. "Give me a moment."

"The doctor is on his way." Jimmy rubbed her back.

"I'll have to get dressed." She tried to rise again. "He can't see me like this. My hair is a mess."

Jimmy held her in place. "Easy now. Take a minute." He watched as she took long, deep breaths. He could feel her heart hammering away, sending reverberations all through her frail skeleton.

"I'm grand," she repeated, her voice stronger now. "Take me over to the bed now, son." He helped her up and guided her carefully across the room. Once he had her tucked up in bed, with an extra cushion to prop her up a little better, her breathing finally calmed.

"How are you feeling?" he asked, after some time.

Ma put a hand to her forehead. "Must have had a

funny turn." She felt both of her cheeks one after the other. "A rush of blood," she said, before taking Jimmy's hand. "I'm grand. Really. Don't be worrying. And there's no need to be wasting money on a doctor."

But Jimmy wouldn't budge on that point, despite his mother's insistence. They were still arguing about it when he arrived. After examining Ma, he asked to speak to Jimmy in private, so they both stepped out onto the landing. The doctor was younger than expected, fresh-faced enough to look like he was still at Trinity, but he seemed as knowledgeable as the rest of them. He told Jimmy the same thing they always said: lungs were tricky, she needed rest, and then she might improve. But the unspoken part was obvious: the odds were against her.

"Would moving somewhere warmer help?" Jimmy asked him. "Somewhere with less damp and rain?"

"Perhaps," was all he would say.

KITTY SEEMED TO be in better form on Wednesday morning, chatting with customers like her old self. But Jimmy could tell her heart wasn't in it. She flinched any time Felix Rourke's name was mentioned, which was regularly enough. He was some kind of commander in the United Irishmen, and all the speculation on the street was that this meant the rebel leader, Robert Emmet, would soon hang. The prospect hung like a cloud over The Liberties; the people appeared to have adopted him as one of their own—*a funny end for a Protestant from St. Stephen's Green,* Jimmy thought.

He wasn't without sympathy for the man. Clearly, Emmet had given up an easy life. He had wealth, status, and prospects, things most people around here would never have, no matter how hard they worked. However, in the end, he hadn't solely risked his own life but that of all those who'd placed their trust in him too. Jimmy kept his opinions to himself, though, merely nodding along when customers told him it was a terrible thing altogether. After the brawl in The White Bull, he'd learned to keep his trap shut. Besides, Kitty was clearly upset about these latest events—more even than what had come before—and he found himself questioning whether the empathy he had developed for the man was because he fancied her.

Then the news came through that afternoon, from travelers coming in off the Naas Road, that Felix Rourke had been hung in front of his own in home out in Rathcoole. It seemed needlessly cruel, especially towards his family. When he comforted a crying Kitty and called the English murdering bastards, he truly meant it.

THERE WAS NO execution the next day, but word came through that two men from Thomas Street were on trial. Jimmy remembered the boy getting pulled out of the crowd at that first hanging, accused of hurling a cabbage. He wondered if the British had simply arrested everyone they could grab on the night of Emmet's uprising, guilty or not. When he said as much to Kitty, she looked at him strangely for a moment before squeezing his hand.

Jimmy felt comfortable enough now to leave Kitty on her own for brief spells while he ran home to check on his mother every couple of hours. Ma had recovered enough to berate him for leaving his stall each time he appeared.

Kitty seemed genuinely concerned when he told her what had happened with Ma, even suggesting a recipe for nettle tea that might help Ma breathe better while she slept. For the rest of the day, Jimmy alternated between convincing himself to ask Kitty out and warning himself to wait. By close of business, he was still in two minds. Kitty seemed to dawdle even after they had packed up, but Jimmy ultimately chickened out. He cursed himself the whole way home, swearing he would proposition her the next day.

And refuse to take no for an answer.

6

B Y THE TIME Friday rolled around, the increased tension in the city was palpable. Thomas Street was jammed at eight in the morning—the biggest crowd so far for a hanging. Jimmy paused to take stock and was almost knocked over by a porter trying to guard his cargo from enquiring hands. Jimmy clipped one of the tykes on the ear. "Go on out of that."

Tipping his cap in thanks, the porter broke free of the bustle and charged towards Crane Lane, as if worried the mob would reel him back in. Jimmy peered back up towards the gallows, where nooses were strung for two today, both local men. John Killen ran a cellar pub at the St. James' Gate end of the street, and John McCann was the well-known proprietor of the scruffy alehouse at the corner of Dirty Lane. Bottled-up anger still surrounded the hanging of Felix Rourke the day before, and mingled with a general sense of foreboding that the rebel leader Robert Emmet would soon be on the chopping block too. Jimmy pushed his way through to where the crowds thinned at the junction of Meath Street. Stopping, he took a breath and mopped his brow, and recognized Kitty coming from the opposite direction. He put his cart down and they stared at each other for a moment, neither saying a word.

Eventually, Jimmy spoke. "You can follow me up, if you like." She looked confused, so he nodded back towards the gallows. "After, I mean."

She stared at him with strange, fierce eyes. "I've seen enough." Turning sharply, she then started walking back the way she had come, towards Cornmarket. "Come on, these bottles won't sell themselves."

He followed, noting the strange, manic edge she had this morning, as if she were a caricature of herself. It disturbed him to begin with, but he soon found himself getting swept up in her infectiousness. But if he didn't know better, he'd have sworn she was drunk. It was as if the last two days had never happened. Kitty began holding his gaze a little longer than usual, or slightly stroking his hand when he passed her something. When she squeezed past him, he swore he could feel her nipples brushing his chest. That excited him so much he almost asked her out on the spot, but she thwarted him by slipping away across the road to Mulligan's, returning triumphantly with a jug of whiskey. "It's Friday," she said, taking a sip and passing it to Jimmy.

The day was unseasonably warm with a near-suffocating level of humidity, the sky threatening to rip itself apart at any moment in one glorious storm. The tension between him and Kitty kept building too. His shoulder tingled when she let her hand rest upon it. Her eyes teased him with each mocking look. Her laugh—deep and throaty when one of the traders shared a bawdy joke, but light and musical when he told one of his own—was driving him demented. With the whiskey flowing through his veins, Jimmy worried he would grab her and kiss her, right there, in front of everyone.

He couldn't take it anymore.

Despite the healthy number of potential customers still milling about Thomas Street, he turned to Kitty. "Let's call it a day."

"You sure?"

"Definite."

Relief flooded her face. She must have known what he was thinking. The two of them raced through the packing up in record time.

"Is that it?" Kitty asked.

Suddenly, Jimmy's nerves returned. "Not quite," he managed. "Can you walk back with me? There's something I want to discuss with you."

Kitty shook her head. "I can't."

"It'll only take a minute."

"I have to go." She looked nervous, flighty even.

Perhaps she's nervous for the same reason, Jimmy thought.

He took her hand. "Kitty." He looked both ways, making sure none of the other traders were eavesdropping. "I've wanted to do this all week, and maybe I shouldn't, but what the hell... Can I take you out for a drink?"

"I can't," she said, without pausing.

Jimmy didn't know what to say to that. At worst, he'd been expecting some hasty excuse, not a flat refusal. St. Catherine's bell tolled in the distance, and Kitty searched it out with her eyes. "I have to go," she said.

She squeezed his hand for a moment and then hurried in the direction of the church, without looking back. Jimmy trudged home, alternating between annoyance at himself for being hasty and confusion at her response.

Nora was there when he returned, and she had already given Ma her dinner.

His mother watched him with that strange expression again. "Wasn't expecting to see you until later," she said, and Nora tittered. He put up with their knowing glances and hinting comments for a few minutes before getting thick and storming out.

Jimmy walked straight to The White Bull. He approached the counter with his eyes fixed on the barman and slammed some coins down. "That's what I owe from last Saturday," he said, leaving just as quickly. He wasn't quite sure what to do with himself next, so he ended up drifting towards Hell, standing at the top of the Forty Steps for what seemed like an eternity, until some drunken old fella shoved him out of the way and staggered down into the darkness.

He turned on his heel and walked down Francis Street instead, going all the way to the end until he reached a small pub with no name at the entrance to Golden Lane. He had already walked beyond it and was heading up towards Blackpitts, with no real destination in mind, when the plaintive sound of *uilleann* pipes followed him up the alleyway. He returned to the pub's window and stared inside, noticing all the smiling faces, the fire glowing in the back. Feeling unworthy of such contentment, he almost turned away again, but right then the heavens finally opened. *A sign from God*, he thought, *telling me to get good and drunk*. Blessing himself, he ducked inside.

HE WAS ON his way home, his head full of dreams, when he spotted her. At first, he thought she was a figment of his imagination. Jimmy rubbed his eyes, but the mirage didn't disappear. It was Kitty all right, scurrying down Ardee Street, clutching a bag tightly to her chest. Questions flew through his addled mind as the rain lashed down. What was she doing out so late on her own?

Jimmy didn't know, but he was going to find out.

He watched as she paused at the corner of Bull Alley, nervously glancing right and left before hurrying down the laneway.

Didn't she say she lived over in Smithfield? Wherever she's going, he realized, *it's not home.*

He ran to the corner and peered down the lane before following at a safe distance.

Jimmy trailed her this way until she came to Christchurch and the entrance to Hell. She surprised him by stopping and blessing herself at the top of the Forty Steps, and she would almost have spotted him if he hadn't managed to blend in with a gaggle of drunkards staggering up Skinner's Row, ducking behind them as they howled at the moon. Once Kitty disappeared from view again, Jimmy ran around the other side of the church and down Fishamble Street, catching his breath in a shadowed doorway as she reappeared at the bottom of the steps. She checked both directions again before crossing the street and heading down Copper Alley. With fear constricting his throat, Jimmy slowly made his way to the corner just in time to see her enter The Maiden Tower—Darkey Kelly's old brothel. Stunned, he turned and walked back up Fishamble Street in a daze, straight into the first bar he saw on Skinner's Row.

He swallowed his pint in huge gulps, desperately trying to control his emotions. *Maybe she was just delivering something. Yes, that must be it.* He signaled for another as his nerves began to ease. These brothels must have laundrywomen and the like, seamstresses repairing dresses and whatnot. *Just because she went in there doesn't mean...* He couldn't even think it, let alone say it. It was only after he had paid for his second that Jimmy realized how expensive the place was. He remembered Fergal's maxim: the closer you get to the Castle, the dearer the drink—one of the few rules, Fergal always claimed, that still applied in Hell.

Fuck it. He took another big draw of stout and wiped his lips on his sleeve. The bar was far more salubrious than anything in The Liberties. While it wasn't the kind of grand establishment the gentry might frequent on Sackville Place, it was fancy enough to put Jimmy on edge. Velvet drapes blocked the window from prying eyes, and a fire raged in an elaborately carved hearth. What really caught the eye, however, was the outsized stag's head taking pride of place above the mantelpiece, its horns thick and strong, its eyes glassy and unknowable. *Must have been some beast,* he thought, wondering if this was the infamous stag's head with which Buck Whaley once settled an account.

Buck Whaley had been a favorite of Da's, an eccentric member of the upper echelons of society who was well liked by all class of men. He'd been famous around Dublin for his outrageous wagers, and infamous for his capacity for drink. Whaley's father had been a severe man whose sole source of amusement was riding around on horseback of a Sunday and torching Catholic churches. He'd died when his only child was just three years old, leaving Buck Whaley an incredible fortune.

Almost inevitably, he turned into a dissolute young man, exclusively occupied with drinking, gambling, and whoring. He bet the Duke of Leinster £15,000 that he could defy the Ottoman Empire, and the *banditti* swarming the region, and visit the Holy Land. Lord

Fitzgerald gave him two years to get to Jerusalem and back, but he did it in half the time. One rather more drunken night, he'd been challenged to leap a carriage parked outside his St. Stephen's Green home—from the second-floor window. He made the leap and survived the fall, incurring only a broken leg; the Arabian steed was significantly less fortunate. Whaley's legend had reached the point where you could make up anything ridiculous about him and people would assume it was true. The story behind the stag's head was a classic example. In the version Da favored, Buck Whaley had attempted to settle his bill at the end of a particularly indulgent afternoon when the proprietor got upset over a minor point regarding some broken chinaware and refused to take credit. Buck Whaley stormed out in a temper, returning later that day with a felled stag as payment.

Jimmy only realized he was staring at the trophy when the barman offered to top up his glass. Waving away the offer, he turned his gaze to the wealthy patrons instead, his lip curling at their affluence. "Life must be grand," he said to himself, "when you never have to worry about money." He hated them all.

Jimmy nearly choked on his drink when Kitty made her entrance. He almost didn't recognize her at first; she had been completely transformed. Her face had been painted in a brazen manner that made her green eyes sparkle all the more. She hesitated on the doorstep a moment, her cheeks flushed as she scanned the crowd. Her royal blue dress and slim figure had already caught the eye of several other patrons, and Jimmy had to control his temper at some of the salacious comments around him. After taking a breath, Kitty stepped forward confidently into the center of the room, and Jimmy slouched over the bar, out of view, rising slowly only when she engaged an impeccably-dressed gentleman in conversation and removed her gloves in a most provocative manner.

When she turned her head, he quickly put his back to the pair, searching for another exit, but there was none.

A tap on his shoulder made him freeze.

"Another?" asked the barman.

He nodded, glancing over towards Kitty again. She was leaning forward, whispering into the gentleman's ear while he stared down her low-cut bodice. Jimmy's gaze followed his, and he couldn't help but also gawp at her powdered cleavage. He watched in horror as Kitty's companion squeezed her left breast; she didn't even flinch.

It was true, he realized. Kitty Doyle was a whore. It

all made sense now: the secrecy, the rejection, the trip to the brothel. She must have been hiding that tart's outfit in the sack she'd been gripping so tightly. He wanted to get out of there immediately, run down to the Liffey and throw himself in its fetid waters—anything to escape the suffocating feeling of dread—but he was trapped. He had no way of leaving without being spotted. They were pawing each other now, that bastard even trying to reach up Kitty's dress, but she took his hand in hers and admonished him. Tugging him towards the door, she beckoned him outside.

Jimmy ordered a whiskey and threw it down his throat. The spirits burned his tongue and made his eyes water, but he instantly waved for another. And then another. By the time he staggered outside, tears stung his eyes and he prayed he wouldn't see the two of them fumbling in some godforsaken alleyway.

7

J IMMY TIPTOED INTO the room, having retained just enough sense to remove his boots before he entered. In his state, the last thing he wanted was a confrontation with Ma. He dropped his boots by the door, almost upending the chamber pot, and quietly slid his straw mattress out from under his mother's bed. Ma didn't even stir.

He lay back and the room began to spin, so he sat up slowly, trying to steady his stomach by fixating on something in the gloom. For a second, he thought he might vomit, but after a few deep, panting breaths his guts unclenched.

Jimmy closed his eyes, and the dizziness returned. Thinking a brief spell in the alley outside in his small-clothes might have a sobering effect, he slowly got to his feet and then shuffled to the door, forgetting the chamber pot and colliding with it in the darkness, spilling its filthy contents all across the floor. His nausea immediately returned. He shot a glance towards Ma, but she still hadn't moved a muscle.

Something wasn't right.

Ma usually had ears like a hawk.

Trying to ignore the foul stench filling the room, he approached the bed, his dread mounting, "Ma?" he called softly.

She didn't respond.

He placed a hand on her forehead. Stone cold. He shook her. "Ma, wake up."

She didn't move.

"Quit joking now." He shook her more vigorously. "Ma." His voice rose into a scream. "Come on, Ma. Wake up!"

He fell to his knees, clutching her hands in his and cried for Ireland. When his sobbing ceased, he kissed her on the cheek and closed her eyes, blessing himself before placing two shillings on her eyelids. Then he scrubbed the floor until dawn.

He made his way to Nora's house in a daze, ignoring anyone who tried to greet him.

His aunt opened the door, still in her nightgown at this early hour. "No!" she cried, her face ashen at the sight of him. Tears streamed down Jimmy's face, but he could only nod silently. "Come in, come in." Nora blessed herself. "Lord have mercy on us. Is it true? Is she gone?"

He nodded again, dumbly, as Nora maneuvered him into the house and sat him down on a stool. Two of her grandchildren sat up, bleary eyed.

"Patrick," Nora said, turning to the older of the pair, "get up to the church and fetch Father Maguire." She threw his breeches at him. "Quick as you can now. Tell him Brigid has passed."

Patrick started crying, and Nora drew him into an embrace. "Shush now, child. It will all be fine. But you need to be strong now for your granny. Go get Father Maguire." The boy nodded and pulled on his trousers before running out the door.

Nora turned to Jimmy. "Are you all right, pet?"

When he didn't respond, she grabbed a bottle of *poitín* from the shelf and poured a healthy measure into a cup. "Sip on that now, love, and get your wits back." She had to guide the cup to his lips but he drank willingly. "That's better," she soothed. "Give yourself a minute."

She left him with the cup and disappeared into the next room to rouse his cousins. Jimmy was only faintly aware of their presence as the rest of them filed into the room, stifling yawns. He barely heard their platitudes as more *poitín* was poured. They took their places in an impromptu circle around him, waiting for him to speak.

"Ma died in her sleep," he said, eventually.

Jimmy's aunt blessed herself and then finally gave way to tears.

Nora was dressed by the time Father Maguire arrived, his shock of unruly red hair and wine-stained vestments at odds with the somber occasion. Jimmy followed the pair to Thomas Street, happy to be told what to do because he didn't have a clue himself. He'd been sleepwalking the whole way home, oblivious to the curious stares of passersby, while the priest muttered in Latin. They entered the cramped room that was his home, and Father Maguire began incanting over Ma's body. Nora got the fire going while Jimmy slumped in the corner, not even moving to join in with the prayers or bid the priest goodbye when he was done.

"You need to eat something," his aunt said, searching the shelves.

"Nothing here." Jimmy's voice was distant, mechanical. "Nothing for me anymore."

Nora grabbed his chin and drew his gaze to hers. "Get yourself together. Put those thoughts out of your mind right now. You need to bury your mother."

After he nodded, she scanned the room once more. "Keep that fire going," she ordered. "I'll be back in minute."

She returned shortly with some smoked pork neck and half a pound of bread. "It's going to be a long day," she said, when Jimmy attempted to refuse. "You'll need your strength."

As he picked at the plate she had prepared, Nora poured herself a drink. "Must have been an awful shock to find her like this when you woke."

Jimmy stared at her for a moment, confused. "She died last night," he said. "I didn't even notice when I got in." He shook his head. "I was so lost in my own world, I didn't notice. Ma was always terrible for the snoring, but she was as quiet as a church-mouse, even when I was bumbling about in the dark."

Nora's eyes welled. "I remember it growing up. Our father always said she could wake the dead with that racket." She took another sip of whiskey and handed the glass over to Jimmy. The smoky peat emanating from the glass reminded him of what he'd been doing all night while Ma had passed, and he let out another anguished cry, this time thinking of Kitty.

Nora took the glass from his hand and hugged him. "Let it all out, Jimmy." She patted his back. "Let it all out."

He was too weak to help bring Ma up to Bully's Acre, the paupers' graveyard behind the Royal Hospital in Kilmainham; instead, he trailed behind his cousins as they carried the corpse, now shrouded in the cloth burial sack, on their shoulders. By the time they arrived, the gravediggers had finished their work and the plot was ready. Father Maguire stood at the head of the grave, a small mound of soil bearing a flimsy wooden crucifix at his feet. The cloth sack containing Ma was placed to one side of the grave. The priest blessed himself and then brought his hands together. "Let us pray."

The service was mercifully brief. Father Maguire had begun a meandering sermon but seemed to lose his way and then wrapped things up quickly, his face nearly as red as his hair. Jimmy summoned enough strength to help lower Ma to her final resting place, but he broke down again when he began shoveling soil down. He was suddenly struck with the thought that they had made some terrible mistake, that Ma was merely sleeping and that he needed to tear open the burial shroud to let her breathe. But he was frozen in place, watching in terror as one shovelful of wet earth after another thumped down onto Ma until there was no white cloth peeking through at all.

He folded into himself, almost curling into a ball, before uncoiling and staring blankly at his cousins as they continued filling the grave. And then he cried. Jimmy never did get to cry for his father—there'd been just the slow, painful realization that Da was never coming home. Ma had always wanted to find his resting place. She'd always said that her one wish was to discover where he was buried and place a flower in his memory. Right then and there, as the last of the earth was patted down, he resolved to fulfill his mother's wish. He would find Da's grave, even if it meant dealing with folk Ma would rather he avoided. *Certain things need to be made right.*

One-by-one, his cousins and other assorted well-wishers filed past and shook his hand as he sat staring at the plot. Then they shuffled silently off, back towards the city. His cousins offered to stay with him and keep watch, but Jimmy insisted on doing it alone. Eventually, they agreed, but not before Patrick had handed over a knife for protection. Fresh graves had to be guarded these days, unless you were rich enough to afford a giant stone slab or a wrought-iron cage. The English plague of bodysnatching had spread to Dublin now too. Surgeons up at Trinity College had an insatiable appetite for fresh cadavers, and the law only granted them the corpses of murderers or of those facing the noose who'd agreed to sell their body. Superstition usually ensured that even desperate men would think twice before taking the coin. Demand was filled by freelancers—gangs who broke into graveyards in the still of night and carted off the newly buried. The newspapers called them 'resurrection men,' but the people of The Liberties had dubbed them 'sack-em-up merchants.'

Jimmy fingered the hilt of the knife. *Let them come,* he thought, *and there'll be plenty of fresh corpses.* The authorities had been scandalized by the recent spate of bodysnatching, but there was little that could be done. The dead were no longer persons in the eyes of the law, and the sack-em-up merchants were wise enough to strip corpses before absconding with them—the dead's clothes being legal property for which a charge of theft could be brought. The courts were powerless. *There's something wrong with the world,* he thought, *when an honest man can't ply his trade because his place of business has been turned into a damned gallows, but he has to guard his mother's grave all night to prevent some thief from selling her corpse.* He sighed and took a sip from the bottle Nora had left him. *Time to leave this accursed island for good.*

He was just starting to doze off when a rustling in the bushes snapped him to attention. Instinctively, his hand gripped the handle of the knife. Drawing it from his belt, he crouched low so his profile wouldn't be visible in the moonlight that bathed the wide, open graveyard. He waited, listening intently. Sweat loosened his grip on the weapon, but apart from a gentle breeze rustling leaves in the distance, the night was silent. Jimmy wiped his hands on his thighs and searched the darkness for movement, wishing he'd accepted his cousins' offers to stand watch. Was it simply a stray dog rooting around? He was on the verge of moving from his hiding spot when he heard the shatter of breaking glass followed by a stifled curse.

He stood erect and stepped out into the moonlight, brandishing his blade.

"Come out, you cowards. Out where I can see you. And you'll know all about it." Something scrambled through the bushes. Jimmy tensed. *Here it comes.* He gripped the knife tighter. "Do your worst," he roared.

The intruder stepped forward into the moonlight, a broken bottle clutched in his right hand. A man with wild eyes that he'd recognize anywhere: Mahaffy.

8

"ONE MORE STEP and I'll gut you." Jimmy circled Mahaffy, blade outstretched.

Mahaffy took a step back. "Put that away now, *gasún*, before someone gets hurt."

"Get back, I said." Jimmy sliced the air in front of him. "And drop your weapon."

"Weapon?" Mahaffy looked at the broken bottle and roared laughing. "I was bringing drink, you eejit. Cracked it climbing over that damned wall."

"I said drop it."

"I'll do more than that." Mahaffy flung the broken bottle away and sat down on the ground, both hands in the air. "Look," he continued, keeping his eyes on Jimmy, "I mean you no harm. I swear it. I came out of respect to your father. I knew you'd be keeping watch tonight." He eyed Jimmy's knife. "Would you ever put that away, for feck's sake?"

Jimmy lowered the blade, but kept his grasp on the

handle tight and both eyes locked on Mahaffy.

"I know your mother wasn't fond of me, not after your father died, at least. But we were friends at one point."

Jimmy snorted.

"It's true," said Mahaffy. "Was even sweet on her once. Don't look at me like that. I courted her before your father came to Dublin."

Jimmy raised an eyebrow. "I thought they came up together, after they got married."

Mahaffy laughed again. "Is that what Brigid told you?" He stared into Jimmy's eyes. "How much do you really know about your father?"

He was lost for words. "Not much," he conceded. "Da was a private man."

"Aye, that he was." Mahaffy looked over at the broken bottle. "Wish I hadn't dropped that bloody whiskey."

Jimmy looked down at the knife in his hand, suddenly feeling foolish. He placed it back in his belt and held a hand out to Mahaffy. "Come on," he said. "I have a drop stashed up here."

The pair sat at the graveside and tore into the drink. It was jocular enough to begin with—shared reminisces of Da's stubbornness while trading sips of whiskey—

until Jimmy prodded Mahaffy about his father's secret.

"I'm not going to dress it up for you," he warned. "And you're not going to like it. I presume your father never spoke about his own parents."

Jimmy shook his head, prompting a grunt from Mahaffy before he continued. "There's good reason for that," he explained. "Your father was the bastard son of a fisherman's wife and someone else's husband."

Jimmy uncorked the bottle and poured a slug of whiskey down his throat. Da had always said his father had died when he was a babe and he didn't have any memory of him. Any time he'd tried to probe further, Da had always changed the subject—Jimmy had assumed out of grief.

"Then why take his father's name? Or is that even true?

"Spite," Mahaffy replied. "His way of picking at the scab, keeping it fresh. That's my guess at least. Myles never did like to talk about it."

"But… why?"

"I'll get to that. Your grandmother's husband had long passed by the time Myles came into the world. He was spared the orphanage, though. She said he was the result of a visitation from the spirit of her dead husband."

Jimmy gave a little cough, but said nothing, instead passing the bottle to Mahaffy for a sup.

After a healthy gulp, Mahaffy continued. "The neighbors indulged this fantasy, calling her a whore only when her back was turned. But she knew what they really thought."

"Then why bother?"

"It's different down the country. Appearances are everything. Your grandmother's charade allowed her to go about her business unmolested, sell milk in the market, take a pew at the back of the church without being hissed at by the other widows. Besides, some of them probably suspected the horrible truth."

"Which was?" asked Jimmy, a tone of exasperation creeping into his voice.

"I'm coming to that." Mahaffy took a breath. "Myles only stayed in Fermoy long enough to bury his mother and then fecked off to Dublin."

"What about the rest of the family? He must have been young when it happened."

"Barely eighteen," Mahaffy replied. "Some of the cousins made a few half-hearted offers to help him get on his feet, but Myles didn't see much point continuing to work land that could barely feed him—not when it wasn't his land to begin with. They were sharecroppers, so there was nothing for your granny to pass on when she died. Myles had no real plan, but no one could stop him: he left the day after the funeral. As he always said, there's more to life—"

"—than milking someone else's cows."

"Precisely."

"I always thought that expression was figurative," Jimmy said somewhat ruefully. "But I still don't understand. Why would my father lie about all this?"

Mahaffy's eyes were downcast focusing on his hands. A pained expression crossed his face. "The story I just told you is the one he first told me. It's true, for the most part. But it's not the whole story." He paused, glancing up at Jimmy. "I don't think his mother gave herself... willingly to that man."

"You mean?"

Mahaffy nodded.

"Jesus Christ." He took another swig. "Then why take this man's name?"

"Grief makes people do strange things. But I think your father had a reason."

"Which was?"

Mahaffy stared at him. "So he'd never forget." He absently picked at a callous on his left thumb. "So he'd never forget that a Protestant could commit the worst sin imaginable against a Catholic and still be beyond the reach of the law."

Jimmy took another swig.

"If you're thinking of revenge," Mahaffy continued, "your grandmother's honor was restored, eventually."

"What do you mean?"

"We got him."

"We?"

"Aye," he said, rubbing his palms together. "And I'll say no more about it."

Jimmy nodded and stared off into the distance. They both sat in silence as the sky began to cloud over; the stars winked out one-by-one.

"I hope you understand now," Mahaffy said. "Why your father had to fight, I mean. He couldn't live in a world where such things were permitted. He was willing to give his life to try and change that. I suspect it's why your mother drew a veil over the past. She wanted to keep you safe. More than likely, she worried you'd come to the same conclusions as your father. It's his blood running through your veins, after all."

Jimmy sat in silence for the longest time. He peered out over the broad sweep of Bully's Acre, picturing all the corpses rotting in the earth. Empty vessels now, but once so full of vitality, real people who had lived and dreamed and suffered.

"I'm leaving," he said, eventually. "But there's one thing I have to do first." He turned to Mahaffy. "I need to know where Da's grave is. As I put Ma in the ground, I promised I'd fulfill her wish to place a flower at his grave. Can you tell me where he's buried?"

"I can do one better," replied Mahaffy. "I can take you there."

IT WAS WELL past four o'clock, and Mahaffy still hadn't appeared. Jimmy would rather have left earlier, but Mahaffy had suggested the early evening would be best, so they could blend in with all the farmers returning home. He'd also promised to procure a horse and cart for the journey south; presumably, this was the cause of the delay. So he waited. And watched.

Wood Quay was busy for a Sunday. Peddlers swarmed around the disembarking seamen, hoping to relieve them of some of their hard-earned pay before they spent it all in Hell. Jimmy had already picked up his own supplies: a wheel of cheese, some bread, a smoked ham, and two bottles of milk from the dairy near Nora's house on the Coombe. Mahaffy had told him to reckon on four days' travel—maybe five, if the weather turned. He yawned, watching another ship casting off from the dock and absently wondering where it was bound. What adventures did he have to come? He tried to picture his own impending voyage, and where it might lead, but his imagination drew a blank. The past still weighed too heavy for any future to be possible.

The sun made its lazy way down to the horizon. Light reflected off the Liffey—a lovely sight, for once, as long as you held your nose. He saw Mahaffy approach, looking for all the world like a sailor about to leave port, a sack over his shoulder and a hunted look in those mad eyes.

"Change of plan," he said gruffly, shaking Jimmy's hand and dropping the sack at his feet. "I can't leave with you, but my driver will take you right to the spot."

He peered over Jimmy's shoulder, squinting into the blinding sun to wave to someone in the distance. Jimmy heard the steady *clip clop* of a horse and cart approaching.

"It's family," Mahaffy said, trying to reassure him. "I trust them implicitly. They know Vinegar Hill well."

Jimmy went to speak, but Mahaffy plowed on, interrupting him. "Everything is arranged, so don't worry. You'll find some food in there, and a blanket if you get cold. And ye have somewhere to stay in Wicklow on the way."

"Why can't you come?"

Mahaffy looked sidelong at him. "I'm being watched," he said, eventually. "It will only cause you trouble, and there are… certain matters I need to handle here in Dublin. But you're in good hands. Trust me." He glanced towards the approaching cart. "Ah, here she is."

"She?"

Mahaffy flashed that wolfish grin of his. "I think you've met my niece."

Jimmy put a hand up to shield his eyes and peered towards the driver.

Kitty Doyle.

"You getting in, or what?" She smiled.

Jimmy climbed aboard, mouth open in shock, and Mahaffy threw him up the sack before slapping the horse's rump. "Safe journey now."

He barely managed a wave in response; his head was spinning. Niece? Of Mahaffy?

Kitty turned to him with what looked like genuine concern on her face. "Are you all right?"

"I'm…" Words abandoned him.

Kitty placed a warm hand on his arm, and it was all he could do not to flinch. "Sorry about your mother. Lord rest her soul." She blessed herself. "It's a terrible thing."

He bit his lip, trying to contain his emotions.

Kitty tugged the reins sharply, turning the horse to avoid an infant crawling in the dirt, its panicked mother scooping the babe up almost too late.

"Are you sure you know how to control this beast?" he snapped.

One corner of her mouth twitched up, and she cracked the reins, tearing down the quays at a frightening pace.

Jimmy rocked back, gripping the cart in sheer panic. "All right, all right!"

She slowed the horse a touch.

"You know what you're doing," he conceded.

"You don't know the half of it." She laughed.

Jimmy bit his lip and then watched the city pass him by. Merchant's Quay gave way to Usher's Quay before Kitty turned them sharply up Watling Street. He worried that she would turn onto Thomas Street, but Kitty veered right onto James' Street instead, towards Kilmainham and the Naas Road.

"We'll turn south beyond Tallaght," she told him. "Less chance of getting stopped."

The gently rolling fields of south Dublin soon gave way to the misty foothills of the Wicklow Mountains. They passed through Kilbride and Crosschapel and

Blessington—places Jimmy had only ever heard of in song. The further south they went, the more familiar the village names became. It puzzled him, until he realized Wicklow was where most of the fighting in 1798 had taken place. And most of the atrocities, he supposed.

Such thoughts helped distract them as the rain got heavier and the sky grew darker. Kitty had stopped trying to engage him in conversation, which was a welcome relief. Neither of them had spoken for some time when the rain finally eased off as they approached Donard.

She nudged him with her elbow. "You're falling asleep," she said softly. "Lie down in the back and get some rest."

"I'm fine."

She slowed her pace. "When's the last time you slept? You look wrecked. May as well get some kip now." She turned to him. "I plan on going all night."

Jimmy lay down in the back, wondering how many fellas she'd said that to before. He shook away the thought and closed his eyes.

9

O N MONDAY MORNING, Jimmy woke to a wide-
open sky, the shocking expanse of blue confusing
him until he realized he was lying in the back of a cart—
one that was no longer moving. He bolted upright.

The cart was at rest in a field, in the middle of nowhere by the looks of it, and the untethered horse
happily munched on grass in the distance. A low stone
wall bordered the road that cut through the land, and
Jimmy could see the gate through which they must have
gained access. A thick hedgerow ran along the other side
of the field, all the way down the slope until it was
swallowed by a thicket of trees. He couldn't see Kitty
anywhere, or any other signs of life for that matter, save a
wisp of smoke from a cottage.

Jimmy stood up for a better vantage point, shielding
his eyes from the rising sun. He could see the farmhouse
now, way off in the distance. Its whitewashed walls shone
brightly, reminding him of the burning sensation the

lime gave your skin if you brushed against it. The thatched roof had seen better days; he wondered how many rats and spiders had wormed their way inside.

He unbuttoned his breeches and took a slash off the back of the cart, taking great pleasure in the arc he could generate from this height. When done, his stomach started to rumble, and he dug out some cheese and bread and stuffed it into his mouth. He stretched out, lying back in the cart again, his hunger sated but his head still foggy.

His whole life had changed in just two weeks. Ma was gone forever. His only 'friend' had abandoned him. The girl he was besotted with, the only one who'd ever shown any real interest in him, was a whore. And now he was trapped with her for the next four days. He knew it would take all his strength not to confront Kitty about what he'd seen. But he had to keep quiet, and he had to forget his interest in her. He had just one more thing to do before he left Ireland for good, and once Kitty had taken him to Vinegar Hill, he could put it all behind him. Start again. The thought of a new beginning filled him with peace. In America, he could be anything. *Anyone.*

Screams cut through his daydreaming. A woman's voice. He jumped to his feet, cupping his ear.

Nothing.

Jimmy pulled on his boots, scanning the area from where the sound had originated, and then jumped off the cart and hurtled down towards the copse of trees at the sloping end of the field. His instinct was to yell Kitty's name, but he thought better of it; he may need the element of surprise. When he reached the tree line, he stopped dead and held his breath, straining his ears for any noise. Dark possibilities flooded his mind. What if she'd gone picking flowers and bumped into the Militia? Or perhaps a lecherous farmer had attacked her while she was looking for drinking water, maybe from the brook he could hear gurgling in the distance. He made his way toward the water, trying to keep his clumsy feet from making too much noise. Leaves rustled to his right. Just wind, but it distracted him nonetheless. He paused, his hand on the hilt of his cousin's dagger, struggling to keep his breathing under control.

Another sound caught his attention: splashing water, right ahead of him.

He pulled the knife from his belt and crept forward as quietly as the autumn leaves would allow. And then he saw her.

Kitty was sitting on a rock beside a small pond, naked, trailing her foot in the water. He could see the side of her breast as she arched her back and shook the last droplets from her hair.

Suddenly feeling guilty about spying on her, he stepped backward. A twig crunched under his boot. Her head whipped around in his direction just as Jimmy hunkered down out of view, praying she hadn't spotted him. He heard another splash as she re-entered the water, and almost blessed himself in relief. When his breathing had calmed, he crept back to his earlier position. Kitty's hair was tied above her head now, and she had paddled into the center of the pond. She rolled onto her back, her breasts breaking clear of the water for one glorious moment.

Jimmy couldn't help taking the Lord's name in vain.

Her head jerked his way again, and he froze, hoping the meager foliage would shield him from view.

"Jimmy," she called. "Is that you?"

Seeing no other option, he stepped into full view, making a show of averting his eyes. "I'm sorry," he said, feeling a flush creep up his neck. "I heard a scream and came running."

"It was freezing!" She laughed, and then paddled towards him, her long limbs ghostly in the water's murk. "But it's after warming up nicely. Are you getting in?"

"What?" Jimmy sputtered.

Kitty laughed again. "I grew up in a house with three boys. I'm sure it's nothing I haven't seen before."

He fought an overwhelming desire to tear off his clothes and jump in the pond, consequences be damned. But his mind kept returning to the man fondling her in that bar on Skinner's Row.

I bet it's nothing you haven't seen before, he thought sourly, barely stopping himself from saying it aloud. "I'll see to the horse." He wheeled away, heading back toward the field, hating himself more with each step.

By the time he had rounded up the horse and tethered it to the cart, Jimmy thought he had his emotions under control. His mind squashed any thoughts of Kitty's naked body as soon as they materialized, but any semblance of control disappeared when she returned, her wet hair glistening in the morning sun, her dress clinging to her slender body. He couldn't help staring as she approached. His mind filled with all the images he had suppressed: the smooth silk of her skin, the curve of her breasts, those rose-colored nipples.

"You better shut that gob before you catch a fly," she said, clambering up onto the cart.

He snapped his jaw shut, and climbed up beside her. Neither said a word as she led the cart out of the field. Jimmy hopped down briefly to open the gate.

"Sorry," Kitty said, when she climbed back on board.

"What for?" He tried not to look at her; that wet hair was driving him to despair.

"I must have given you an awful shock."

He glanced up briefly to see her eyes dancing in that gently mocking way. "Waking up in the field on your own." The corners of her mouth curled upward.

"Oh… right," stammered Jimmy. "Of course."

Barely another word was spoken until they reached Baltinglass.

She surprised him by not stopping in the town itself, but Jimmy thought it best not to ask questions, keeping any interaction to a minimum—not an easy task when traveling alone with somebody. A couple of miles beyond Baltinglass, they turned down a tiny *boirín* that seemed to stretch on forever. The road, if it could be called that, was barely wide enough for the cart and was hemmed in on both sides with thick hedgerows. He wondered what the hell they would do if they met someone coming the other way. After traveling in silence for a fair stretch, they came to a fork in the road. Kitty deliberated for some time, even getting off the cart to walk a little way down each path. Finally, she elected to go left. Jimmy didn't say a word throughout the whole episode.

The road rose gently at first, soon becoming steeper

and steeper. After several miles, the tired mare required much cajoling to keep going, but eventually the hill crested and the *boirín* opened out into a yard with a low, thatched cottage on the left and a barn further back. The farmhouse looked a far more solid affair than the one Jimmy had seen earlier. The thatch had obviously been replaced sometime within the last year, its bristle-edges neat and trimmed, and the walls beneath were gleaming. Casting a shadow from a considerable distance at back of the yard was the hay barn, which contained more than enough feed for the winter. A scattering of hens pecked the dirt in front, paying no heed to the intruders.

Kitty leaped down from the cart and patted the horse's nose. "Sorry for the climb, but you can rest now for a couple of days." She turned to Jimmy, who stood watching, one eyebrow raised. "We'll change horses here and pick this girl up on the way back," she explained.

"Oh."

"But we'll stop here for the night, unless you have any objection to sleeping in a real bed."

"No, none at all."

"If we get to bed early and leave at dawn tomorrow, we could be at Vinegar Hill before the day is out."

He tried to muster some false cheeriness. "Perfect, thank you." He looked around. "Where is everyone?"

"Working, I imagine." She tilted her head toward the darkening sky. "But I'd say we'll see them soon enough. Come on, let's get inside. It's starting to get cold."

Jimmy paused.

"Don't worry, silly." She took his hand. "They're family."

His heart quickened at her touch, and he shook his hand free, ignoring the wounded look on her face as the door of the cottage opened.

"Look who it is!" A woman of around fifty stepped out into the yard, and Kitty ran toward her. "Oh, it's wonderful to see you," she said as they embraced. She peered past Kitty to Jimmy, eyeing him sharply up and down. Squeezing Kitty's arms, she asked, "Who's this, then?"

"A friend," replied Kitty, stressing the latter word. "Jimmy." She turned to him. "Jimmy, this is my aunt Maeve."

"Pleasure to meet you." He shook the woman's outstretched hand.

"He's from Dublin," she said, "but don't hold that against him. We're on our way down to Vinegar Hill, and we were hoping to impose on you for the night."

"Of course, of course. You'll want to give this poor girl a rest, I imagine." Maeve gestured to the horse, which was still blowing from its efforts up the steep road.

"If you can spare a horse."

"It's no bother at all. You don't even have to ask." She smiled. "Especially if it means I get to see you again on the way back."

Kitty laughed. "I hoped you'd say that."

"You know you're always welcome here." She pinched Kitty's cheek. "Now, have you any news."

"Plenty, but we'll save that for later."

Jimmy noticed an almost imperceptible look pass between them. Maeve nodded. "Right you are. Let's get inside." Maeve turned to him. "You must be famished. I'll show you where you can wash up, and then we'll see about some dinner."

10

THEY PULLED OUT the next morning with a fresh horse and Kitty loosened off on the reins as they made their way down the *boirín*. She thought back to the knowing look her aunt had given her as she'd climbed up beside Jimmy on the cart that morning. Kitty's face had flushed with embarrassment at her aunt's obviousness, but Jimmy hadn't noticed. He seemed just as morose and distant as usual. She tried to remind herself that he'd just lost his mother and was on the way to visit his father's grave for the first time. Anyone would be upset under similar circumstances, but something about his demeanor kept niggling at her.

Last night, for example, he'd been perfectly friendly to Maeve, even charming at times, but was curt whenever she had tried to speak with him. Kitty knew she wasn't imagining it. Her aunt had remarked on it too, once Jimmy went to bed.

Kitty didn't tell Maeve she suspected he'd been

watching her swim yesterday. Her face reddened again as she remembered her audacious manner when she'd invited him to join her. Was that what was bothering him? Had she been too forward? Jimmy did seem a little prudish, but that could also be shyness. Perhaps he was used to quiet women, who waited for a man to take the initiative. That wasn't her. And, sure, wasn't he all over her last week? Didn't he near pant like a dog when they'd been working together?

Men. She harrumphed, needlessly slapping the reins again. She could live a thousand years and never figure them out. Perhaps it was because she'd refused him last Friday? Males were typically proud creatures, in her experience, but Jimmy had seemed different—almost sensitive, in a way. She admired how he'd looked after his mother when it was perfectly clear he wanted to leave Ireland. Most would have palmed her off onto a relative and left regardless. But he stayed. Once again, the thought surfaced—the foolishness of chasing a man who was talking about leaving—but she pushed it away. *One hurdle at a time*, she reminded herself.

When her uncle asked her if she'd accompany Jimmy to Vinegar Hill, Kitty had almost jumped out of her skin. She feared she must have blushed when he'd suggested pretending to be man and wife if they were stopped by the Militia.

"I thought you suspected him," she'd said.

"Well, I don't anymore," was all her uncle would say. And it was all Kitty could do to hide her relief. It was a strange business, rooting around in a man's life, trying to discover whether he was an informant. Let alone developing feelings for him even before you knew for sure. She had felt guilty about that, until her uncle had agreed with her assessment. For her part, she'd strongly suspected his innocence from the start. Jimmy might have some confused feelings about the rebels—no doubt tied up with the loss of his father—but it didn't make him a traitor.

She thought over what Maeve had said the night before, once Jimmy had gone to bed and Kitty had given her aunt all the news from Dublin, along with the message for the local rebel commander, Michael Dwyer.

"Rein in your feelings," Maeve had warned her. "I've seen you looking his way, all moon-eyed."

"I know what I'm doing," Kitty had protested in reply.

Maeve's eyes softened. "I don't doubt that at all, *a chroí*," she said. "It's him I worry about."

Those words had echoed in Kitty's head all night. She glanced across at Jimmy. He was still staring straight ahead, sullen as a smarting child. She went to reach for his hand, but his reaction the day before stopped her. "What are you thinking about?" she asked, before she could stop herself.

He blinked a couple of times. "Oh, nothing."

The silence that followed was punctuated only by horse's hooves. After a minute of holding her tongue, she decided to press him again. "We've a long way to go, Jimmy. Why don't you tell me what's troubling you?"

His eyes narrowed, as if he was deciding whether to be upfront with her, and then his frown faded, his expression relaxed. "I was remembering the last time I was in a cart like this." He looked up to the sky and Kitty let him find the words. "It's my fondest memory of Da. He got a loan of a horse and cart one day—I think some ragman owed him a debt, people often owed him money. He could never say no to a hard luck story, Ma always said."

He swallowed, as if fighting for control of his emotions, and then continued. "I was only thirteen or fourteen, so the idea of heading all the way out to Malahide was very exciting. Those twelve miles into the countryside seemed like the biggest adventure in the world." He laughed. "I suppose it was, too. First time I'd left Dublin, unless you count Tallaght. And I hadn't left since then, until this here journey."

"Anyway," he continued, "it was a real adventure, especially for a young fella. We took the coastal road, stopping by the old lead mine at Clontarf first. Da reckoned that was the spot where Brian Boru defeated the Vikings. He was always trying to teach me things."

Kitty could see he was starting to well up. This time, she did reach for his hand. He didn't pull away either, even if he did flinch slightly.

"Sheds lined the sea—little wooden shacks right there on the stony beach. Da said they housed the local fishermen. Then he pointed to the fancy-looking taverns we passed and I gazed through the windows at all the people in their finery, shucking oysters from their ridiculous shells. Or trying to, at least."

Kitty made a face, and Jimmy laughed before going on. "We continued on by the marshes at Baldoyle and waved at the craggy peak of Ireland's Eye in the distance, and then passed the brickworks at Portmarnock. Just before we got to the outskirts of Malahide village, Da pulled into the woods and tied the horses. I had no idea what he was planning, which made it all the more exciting. We crept through the thick forest and he picked up a couple of sturdy branches and handed me one. After practicing with our swords, we made for the castle itself.

Da said we were going to break into the feckin' thing and liberate it for the people of Ireland. We just wanted to get a look at it, of course, but it was fun to pretend."

Kitty couldn't help herself. She squeezed his hand, which resulted in him giving gave her a strange, pained look. When he brushed a tear from his eye, she thought her heart would break.

"We were fighting our way through this dense forest one moment," he went on, "and the next, we tumble out into the biggest, wide-open clearing you've ever seen. And right in the middle, was this castle. A proper castle, not like that pile of shite in the center of Dublin. Smaller than I'd imagined, but magical in its own way. Of course, as soon as we were out in the open, a horse galloped towards us: the groundskeeper—a bad-tempered fella by the name of Coghlan—waving this ropey-looking old musket. Rust on it and all. It probably didn't even work, but we couldn't take the chance. He ran us off the grounds, threatening to throw us in the dungeon for poaching."

"What did you do?"

"Ah, we just legged it through the forest. We knew he couldn't follow us on horseback. Da roared with laughter the whole way back to where we'd stashed the cart. 'Don't mind him,' he said. 'That fella Coghlan is famous for being a prick. Thinks he owns the place.'"

Jimmy smiled to himself. "Instead, we went down to the estuary and watched the salt harvesters working away in the sun, boiling off the sea water in these giant iron pans. Da was delighted when one of them told him Malahide used to be a Viking base. He was mad for the history."

"That's a nice memory," Kitty said. "You must treasure it."

Jimmy slipped his hand from hers. "On the way home, he told me he was going off to war."

He stared straight ahead, and Kitty bit her lip, feeling like a prize fool. Why did she have to say anything? She joined him in silence, letting the clopping hooves lull her thoughts into nothingness.

"How will you know where he's buried?" Jimmy finally spoke, some time later.

She cleared her throat. "Because they're all buried in the same place."

KITTY COULD FEEL Jimmy's eyes tracking her as she wandered about, trying to get her bearings. She looked down onto Enniscorthy below, desperately trying to remember. Tendrils of smoke reached lazily towards the sky. A pair of fishing boats bobbed on a river swollen with rainfall. *Maybe that's why God is so blind to our suffering*, she thought. From this distance, the town looked so peaceful. There was no indication of how many had died on that bridge; the blood had long been washed from the cobbles. No monuments stood to remember the dead either, nor was there any other outward sign of the havoc that had been wreaked. Down on the streets, you could see it—in people's eyes, in their shifting gait, their haunted expressions. Not from up here.

She shook her head, not wanting to remember what she was trying to forget.

"You sure you know where it is?" Jimmy asked. "Don't tell me we came all this—"

"Shush and let me think." After a couple of moments, she turned back to him. "They call it The Battle of Vinegar Hill, but it wasn't much of one. The English general brought in four columns of troops—twenty thousand, all told—and tried to trap the Unitedmen on Vinegar Hill. They began shelling immediately. Only the late arrival of one of the columns gave the rebels any chance to run for it. Needham's Gap, they called it, named for the commander whose lateness prevented an even worse slaughter."

Kitty turned westward, toward Enniscorthy. "Those who did escape struck out for the woods east of the River Slaney, eventually making it to Wicklow." Her eyes followed the curve of the river as it encircled the hill to the north. She stepped northwards toward the edge of the bluff. "Which means it should be down here."

She strode up to the crest of the hill, not waiting to see if he was following, and peered downwards. The mound her uncle had previously shown her was immediately obvious. Jimmy came to her side and saw what she was staring at. He fell to his knees, clutching the sad bunch of wildflowers he had picked on the way up. Then he flung them to the ground. There was no need to place them; the mound was covered with vivid blooms.

Blood is the best fertilizer, Kitty thought, watching Jimmy's face contort with pain. She sat down beside him, brushing off her skirt. When he began to cry, gently at first, and then louder, she put her arm around him, hesitantly pulling him into an embrace. His tears were warm on her neck, his body convulsing with sobs, as all the pain he'd carried with him for so long found a voice.

Kitty knew exactly what he was feeling. She almost felt like sharing her own anguish, but something stopped her. She pulled back to look at him. Eyes puffy with tears, he wiped his nose on back of his sleeve. "Sorry," he muttered.

"Don't—"

Then he kissed her.

Kitty almost resisted, but then she fell back on the long grass, taking him with her. He moved on top of her, his kiss deepening, his hands on her face one moment and nervously cupping her breasts the next. She parted her legs, drawing him even closer.

"I can't." Jimmy pulled away and sat up, panting. He stared down at the flower-covered mound; his wet eyes almost as red as Kitty's crimson face. She turned away, biting back an acerbic response. With a deep breath, she rose to her feet. Jimmy didn't even try to stop her. Keeping her emotions in check, she set off down the hill, leaving him to stew in whatever bitter juices flowed through his veins instead of blood.

11

JIMMY WOKE THE next morning with his lips still tingling from yesterday's kiss, more confused than ever. Kitty hadn't spoken more than two words to him since. She'd rejected his entreaties, setting up camp last night in stony silence. He had been embarrassed when she'd laid out a blanket for him beside the fire before going to sleep on the cart by herself. She hadn't even responded when he offered to trade places.

Awake for hours, he'd been, staring at the stars, wondering what kind of skyhooks held them in place. At one point, when he saw one shoot across the sky, he'd almost called out to tell Kitty, but something stopped him. Sitting up, he'd peeked at the cart, breathing a sigh of relief when he saw she was still asleep. Jimmy hadn't been quite ready to face her.

He still wasn't sure if he was ready.

Nevertheless, he stood, seeing no sign of movement from Kitty. Her face was so serene, as she slept there on the cart. His eyes traveled lower. His mind couldn't help but imagine her lithe body under the blanket. Clenching his fists, he stalked away, wondering how he would get through the next two days without having the very conversation he knew he must avoid.

At the edge of the bluff, he gazed down over Enniscorthy, curious how many people down there were wrestling with dilemmas of their own. He knew his feelings for Kitty were real—the kiss had confirmed that much—but couldn't untangle the rest. Absently, he plucked daisies from the ground, tossing each away in turn, wondering if this was how the King of England felt when planning his wars.

He was in love with her, he finally admitted to himself, watching a cloud inch its way across the sky. But he also knew what she was: a whore. He couldn't marry a whore.

Or could he?

Jimmy indulged the fantastical notion for a moment. Who was left to judge him? And who would know or care if he took her to America anyway? If her life was so desperate that she had to prostitute herself to get by, surely she'd happily run away with him. The plan was so seductive it almost seemed viable—until he thought of all the men she must have slept with. The idea disgusted him. Countless greasy paws all over her body. He almost retched.

"You're awake."

He didn't turn. "Aye." He decapitated another daisy, and then stood and tossed the rest away. "I'm sorry about yesterday," he said, turning to face her.

Her expression hardened. "We best get going, while the sky is clear."

Jimmy clambered aboard the cart without another word.

All the way back to Baltinglass, Kitty sat rigid at the reins, barely grunting in response to his pathetic attempts at conversation. It felt like they were both counting down the hours until they could part. At first, he felt guilty. But it was soon replaced with anger. What did she expect? She was a prostitute. A whore. Did she think he'd never find out? The idea enraged him. What kind of fool did she think he was?

He kept his temper in check until they reached the entrance of the *boirín*.

"We have to change horses. Do you want to rest here for the night or keep on?" Kitty asked. It was nothing but an innocent question, but Jimmy exploded out of nowhere.

"What do you care where you sleep?" he snapped.

"What's that supposed to mean?"

He stared straight ahead, silent, clenching his jaw.

Kitty let the horse have its head, and it whinnied as it continued up the *boirín* toward the farmhouse. After less than fifty yards, she yanked on the reins. "What is wrong with you?" she demanded, as the horse planted its feet, rocking the cart. "One minute you're all over me, and the next you won't say two words. I know your mother died, and I'm very sorry about that."

He stared up at the sky in response, exhaling slowly through his nose.

"Jesus Christ, Jimmy, what is it? I threw myself at you, and now I'm mortified ... which is fine. If you don't like me, it's my own fault for getting the wrong impression. But unless I'm going mad, you were doing a fierce good impression of a fella that fancied me. Especially when you bloody well kissed me."

He turned to meet her imploring stare. "I saw you," he said through gritted teeth. "Last Friday. In that bar on Skinner's Row. I saw you."

Kitty's face dropped.

"I knew it," he said. "It *was* you. I've been going mad these last couple of days, wondering if I was mistaken. But it's true. I wasn't entirely sure until just this moment. Maybe part of me didn't want to believe it. Now I know."

She cracked the reins, and the horse broke into a stiff trot up the hill. "You don't know anything," she said, finally. "Nothing at all."

They continued in silence until they reached the farm.

"How are you, my dear?" Maeve's first concern when they arrived was for Jimmy.

"I—"

"He's not feeling the best," Kitty interrupted. "And he'd like to be alone. So let's show him to his room and settle down for a good chat."

Jimmy bit back a reply, and then realized she was doing him a favor. The kitchen table conversation would be impossibly awkward otherwise. He dragged his sack into a room that had been prepared for him and stared out the window, listening to the muted murmurs of the two women coming from the kitchen, their voices animated one moment but hushed the next. When he finished seething, he went to the door and opened it a crack. Even straining his ears, he struggled to make out most words, although he was sure his name was mentioned. He opened the door wider and crept down the hallway.

"This is for your uncle," he heard Maeve say.

"Michael replied?" Kitty asked.

"Aye, just in time, but I get the feeling it's not the answer you're looking for."

Jimmy crept up closer, straining to listen, trying to be as silent as possible.

Kitty spoke so softly he could barely hear her, as if her voice was about to break. "So he's just going to let him die?"

"Quiet now, child. What can he do? Gallop into Kilmainham Gaol and spring him from his cell? Think about it. Deep down, you must have known it would end like this. There's no other way."

Jimmy bit his lip and tiptoed back to the bedroom.

KITTY KNOCKED ON his door before dawn. "Leaving soon," she barked.

His eyes flicked to the door handle, but she had already stomped angrily away. It wasn't quite the fantasy he'd conjured up in his sweaty, fevered sleep, pining for her to come to him in the night.

Jimmy threw off his blanket, exposing his body to the brisk morning air.

This was what I wanted, he reminded himself. *Not to get involved.*

He swung his legs out of the bed, his teeth chattering, and rubbed his gritty eyes with the heel of his palms. Grabbing the wooden jug from the sideboard, he then splashed his face, his stubble bristling against his hands as the water dripped down his chest.

Another knock came on the door.

"Coming," he called, a little too harshly, already pulling on his shirt.

Maeve did her best to keep things friendly over the rushed breakfast, and Jimmy was glad for the eggs. His stomach had been growling all night while he tormented himself with thoughts of Kitty and their impossible future. Once the plates were cleared, Jimmy went to relieve himself in the yard. The sky was grey above, and he turned his eyes up to the clouds, wondering if it would rain now or later. Rubbing his arms, he trudged back to the cottage, dodging a cowpat at the last moment. At the door of the kitchen he paused, watching the easy way Maeve had with Kitty, wishing he could have that with her too.

Kitty caught his eye, and her face scrunched up momentarily before relaxing into a neutral expression.

Maeve squeezed her niece's hand, blurting out, "Probably should get going before it starts raining." She rose to her feet. "I'll see to your horse."

Kitty almost upended her chair to join her.

Jimmy was left alone, staring at an empty table. He swatted away a fly and pushed back from the doorframe, wandering around the side of the cottage toward the hay barn. The clatter of hooves sounded as their horse was led from the stables, and he made his way toward the noise. Kitty and Maeve were deep in conversation again.

Maeve's eyes snapped to him as he approached. "Did you leave that back door open?" she asked. "The pigs'll be in."

"Sorry." Jimmy raced back to close it, deciding to give them a few minutes before returning.

When he did, Kitty was already on the cart. He climbed up alongside her and waved goodbye to Maeve as the horse began to trot down towards Baltinglass, the two of them in the cart still avoiding each other. After they passed through the village, Kitty surprised him by turning northwest, toward Kildare. She didn't explain why. They cut up through various *boírins* and laneways, even shortcutting through a field at one point before landing on the Dublin road somewhere beyond Kilteel. Jimmy wasn't sure why they were taking such a circuitous route home, but he remained silent. He had his theories. Maybe she was avoiding the Militia—everyone in Wicklow seemed to know their movements in advance. Or perhaps she was angry with him and wanted to prolong his suffering. Still speculating, he dozed off in his seat.

Jimmy awoke when the cart came to a halt somewhere he vaguely recognized. He rubbed his eyes and stretched. Beside him, Kitty was as still as an English statue. He yawned and scratched his arms, having enough manners to turn his head away. The yawn immediately died in his throat. Four dead men swayed on the gallows before them. He turned to Kitty, but she had already jumped down off the cart.

Flies buzzed around the putrid bodies, which he guessed were strung up the day before, the English having left them up there to rot. A warning. One that must be heeded.

A small knot of people stood staring at the gallows, watching from a good fifteen feet away. Jimmy wondered whether some invisible barrier kept them back; then he realized it was the stench. Kitty clambered back up onto the cart, clutching her nose, her eyes wide as she stared at the rotting corpses.

"Nicholas Farrell, Laurence Begley, Thomas Donnelly, and Michael Kelly," she said after a moment.

Jimmy was about to respond, when a voice behind him yelled, "That's not Laurence Begley."

He turned to see a woman of about forty with dark circles under her eyes. "It's my John." She blessed herself. "God rest his soul."

"I don't understand," said Kitty.

The widow dabbed the corners of her eyes. "My husband, John Begg, was up for murder, but the court threw out the case. He was acquitted last week, only they forgot to release him. Then, when it came time to hang Laurence Begley…" She let out a strangled cry. "How can someone make a mistake like that?" The poor woman shook her head and turned back to face her dead husband.

Kitty urged the mare forward, and they left Palmerstown behind.

Jimmy tilted his head back into the wind, willing it to blow the cobwebs from his mind, but his thoughts kept returning to that widow, to her pain. To be given hope like that, and then to have it snatched away so callously. He simply couldn't fathom how devastating that must be. He remembered his Da: how he used to come home from a night out, his eyes all glassy. Ma pretending to be cross with him, but really only putting it on. Da would bring him down to the yard and point out all the stars. He made up most of the names, but that was half the fun.

"That one there, that was put up there by a king in Persia," Da would say. "Know where that is? No? Neither do I. East, they tell me," and he'd laugh. And before Jimmy had time to question any of that, he'd be onto the next thing, and then the next, laughing at his own tangents, his eyes burning with passion. Sometimes, Jimmy didn't even listen to the words; he just watched Da's shining face.

KITTY NUDGED HIM awake as they approached the outskirts of Dublin. He stifled his yawns, eyeing her sidelong, trying to avoid another confrontation and wondering how long he'd been dozing. When they approach Kilmainham, he asked to be let off at Bully's Acre. She took off as soon as he disembarked, his thanks swallowed up by dust. Shaking his head, he went to find Ma.

At the gate to the graveyard, Jimmy gave the old fella with the milky eyes a penny and took his blessing. He walked among the tombstones. Mourners were scattered here and there, standing morosely at various graves in the distance; some with family, but most alone. Bully's Acre was shabbier by day. At night, the mist hid the broken flagstones and crooked graves. Sunlight exposed the neglect, reminding him that even those lucky enough to have someone mourn their death and tend their grave would eventually be alone. Their mourners would one day tire of the task, or die themselves. He pinched the bridge of his nose, and two tears squeezed loose.

Fresh flowers adorned Ma's grave. Marigolds or posies, he couldn't remember the name. His mother would have known. She knew the names of every shrub and bush from here to Tipperary. Not only that, she could write a thesis on the soil they best grew from, one that would make a Trinity student proud. Someone had cleaned around the plot too. *Nora must have been by.* In his grief-stricken state, he'd forgotten to let his aunt know he was heading away for a few days. He resolved to call in later, in case she was worried.

Sitting down beside the grave, he stared at the sunny yellow petals. "Ma," he murmured, after some time. "I found Da's grave." Tears slid down his cheeks. "And it was beautiful. The whole place was covered with flowers. You would have loved it."

He looked around Bully's Acre again, watching some fella with a fiddle at the far end of the graveyard. The mourner was staring down at ground as he played.

"I hope you're together now," he said, trying not to

cry. He blinked up at the sky, drawing in great, heaving breaths. Once his heart calmed, he wiped his face.

Two rows down, an elderly lady searched for a grave, making Jimmy suddenly feel stupid for mumbling to the ground. He waited until she was a little farther away.

"I'm leaving, Ma. I have to. I could explain why, but I think you know." He stood, brushing off his breeches. "It will take a few days to organize everything, but I'll be back to see you tomorrow. We'll talk more then."

He kissed his palm and pressed it to the earth, and then he turned, thanked the blind custodian again on leaving, and headed home, walking toward Bow Lane.

Before he even got there, some cheeky brat was trying to flog him an old broadsheet for twice the price. The headline caught his eye: "EMMET TRIAL DATE SET."

He thrust a ha'penny into the beggar's palm, ignoring his feeble complaints, and began reading greedily. The rebel leader, Robert Emmet, was to have his day in court on Monday. *The Crown must have everything they need.*

His eyes flicked to a box in the right-hand corner of the page. Another leading figure in the United Irishmen, Thomas Russell, had been arrested. *There goes Emmet's chance of getting sprung.* His mind clouded over. *All these men throwing their lives away.*

When will it end?

12

"JIMMY!" NORA GASPED when she opened the door to him, panting and red-faced as he was.

"I'm sorry," he managed after a breath or two. "I should have told you I was going away for a few days."

"Where were you?"

"Vinegar Hill," he explained, leaving out any mention of Kitty. He had arrived home yesterday evening to find the place had been cleaned, confusing him until he remembered Nora had a key. He'd lain down on the fresh, clean bedsheets for just a moment, swearing he'd get up and call on his aunt soon, but had fallen asleep instantly, jolting awake this morning with a start. Now he felt guilty. He had pulled on his trousers and boots and raced downstairs, racing the whole way over to The Coombe.

"Come in," she said, ushering him inside before he could argue.

"Scat," Nora told his cousins, after he'd greeted them

all. "Make yourselves scarce for a minute, would you." As soon as they had the room to themselves, she fixed him with a look that instructed him to tell her everything. "How did you get down there?"

"A friend," was all he said at first. But that didn't satisfy her. Before she could pepper him with questions, he stretched. "If I never have to sleep in the back of a cart again, I'll be a happy man."

Nora embraced him fiercely. "Oh, Jimmy. I didn't know where you had gone. I worried something had happened to you. Or that you'd just fecked off without saying goodbye to us."

"Sure where would I go?"

She pulled back, looking him dead in the eye. "America."

"Perhaps," he conceded; there was no point denying it. "But I'd never leave without saying goodbye."

"Promise?"

Jimmy sighed. "Of course."

"You're a good boy." She patted his cheek. "But you're not telling me everything. You've already decided to leave, haven't you?"

Jimmy nodded. His aunt smiled again, but this time her eyes filled with tears.

"Don't cry," he said. "There's been enough crying lately."

Another tear made its way down her cheek, and she laughed. "Sorry."

"It's going to take a few days to figure everything out, but I'll let you know as soon as I do."

"Thanks." She stood and searched for a handkerchief, dabbing her eyes before loudly blowing her nose.

"Sorry for worrying you. There's enough to be dealing with. I wasn't thinking."

"I understand, pet."

"I meant to call over yesterday evening, when I got back, but I collapsed into bed at the sight of it. Thank you for cleaning up."

"That reminds me." Nora took a tin from the shelf and placed it on the table. "How do you plan to pay for a ticket?"

He sighed. "I've been trying to save all summer."

Nora's nostrils flared.

"I've been thinking about this for a while," he admitted. "I wanted to take Ma with me. I thought the warmer weather might be good for her lungs. But with everything that went on, I was just scraping by. I suppose it's the free boat, like Donal, and a contract to work off once I get there."

"Oh, Jimmy. I wish you'd talked to one of us." She emptied the tin onto the table. Six guineas, their golden sheen gleaming unnaturally against the worn kitchen table. His eyes bulged. "Brigid was keeping this for you. She'd saved for years. Hoped to give it to you on your wedding day."

Jimmy stared at the coins. More than enough for a ticket. "How…?"

"Most of it came from your father. He'd always intended it as your inheritance. But your mother diligently added to it whenever she could."

"I thought she was giving all the money to you, for the kids."

Nora shook her head. "Here." She gathered the guineas from the table and held out her hand. "It's all yours now."

He stared at the coins, open-mouthed in disbelief.

"You better write to us when you're over there," she scolded.

"I don't know what to say."

"You don't have to say anything. Just make sure you put it somewhere it won't be found."

"I will."

"I don't mind holding onto it for a bit longer, if you like. It's safe here. There's enough of us that someone is always home. I worry about that room of yours, what with all that's been going on around Thomas Street these last few days."

"What happened?"

"Oh, it's like July all over again. The Militia kicking down doors, smashing furniture. Major Sirr strutting about the place, carting people off to Kilmainham Gaol for no reason at all. It's terrible."

"Is it something to do with the trial on Monday?"

"I don't know. All I heard was that someone was murdered over the weekend. Together with Russell's arrest and Emmet's trial, it's all people are talking about."

"Must have been someone important."

She lowered her voice. "This is just gossip, now, but I heard it was a spy."

"That'd explain it, all right."

"Anyway," she said, "you won't have to deal with this nonsense too much longer." She smiled wistfully. "I envy you—do you know that? And Donal. If I was your age, I'd been gone in a flash too."

"Really?"

"I would. I love Dublin, I do. It's part of me now. But sometimes I think there's too much history here, and we're all struggling to grow in its shadow."

Jimmy knew exactly what she meant.

"Come here to me," she said, tugging him into her

embrace. "Enough of this gloomy talk. What about this young one you were after?"

KITTY CALLED BY the Cornmarket stalls on the way to her meeting. All the traders were there. All except for Jimmy. The others hadn't seen him since last Friday, but they mentioned his mother had passed away. They expected him back at work soon, they all told her, and they were a little surprised he hadn't set up today, it being a Saturday.

"It's a terrible thing to be alone in this world," said Paulie Grogan, leering at her. She ignored him and continued on down Thomas Street.

Stopping opposite Jimmy's building, she peered up at the top floor window, wondering if he was inside, looking out at her. She stuck out her tongue just in case, and then continued in the direction of St. James' Gate, ducking into an alleyway just beforehand. She knocked on the door and was led into the back room of The White Bull, where Mahaffy was waiting.

Kitty eyed the whiskey bottle. "Bit early, isn't it?"

"Sit." He brought the glass to his lips and took a slow draw, eyeballing her the entire time. "I've had a tough few days," he said, glancing away and letting the tension dissipate. "It's a good thing you left Dublin when you did. Major Sirr has been turning The Liberties upside down."

"I won't do anything like that again."

Mahaffy stared at her for a moment. He was so unlike his sister Maeve: hard where she was soft, cynical where she was generous, and ruthless where she was charitable. But Kitty would never forget that it was her uncle who had taken her in without hesitation, when others might have shirked the commitment.

"You won't have to," he said. "Trial is on Monday. Which means they have everything they can get."

"Do you think he talked?"

He shook his head. "I can't see it. They didn't pick up any more of our men, and they would have no reason to wait. Not now."

"Good." She thought for a moment. "What about Anne Devlin? Any word of her being released?"

Mahaffy shrugged.

"But why hold on to her? Surely, the whole point was to get Emmet to talk. That didn't work, or we would know, as you said. What good is she to them?"

"I don't know, to be honest. We're hoping she will be released after…" He splayed his hands. "Did you get a reply from Dwyer?"

Kitty handed over the letter. "You're not going to like it."

"I know what it says already. He can't endanger his men. He's held out for five years in the mountains by not taking unnecessary risks. His first duty is to them."

"Then why ask?"

"We don't have many things left to try here, love. But I had to try."

She looked at the bottle. "Got another glass?"

Mahaffy went through to the bar, leaving her alone with her thoughts for a moment. She wasn't looking forward to the next part of the conversation, but a drink would help.

He returned and handed Kitty a glass. "How did it go with the O'Flaherty boy?"

"Fine." Kitty grabbed the bottle and poured herself a healthy measure. She took a sip. "There's just one thing."

"Oh?"

"He saw me."

"What do you mean?"

Kitty sipped again, hoping the spirits would keep her voice from shaking. "On Friday night, in the pub on Skinner's Row. He saw me."

"Shit." Mahaffy leaned back in his chair, scratching

his stubbly chin. His eyes were locked on Kitty. "What did you say?"

"Nothing."

"Good."

She slowly drained her glass, flinching as it burned her throat. "He thinks I'm a whore," she said in a low voice.

Mahaffy leaned across the table. "Kitty, listen to me. You can't tell him."

She bit her lip; held her tongue. There were plenty of things she wanted to say, but none of them would help. "I know," she said eventually.

"You can't," he insisted.

Kitty slammed the glass down. "I fucking know, all right?"

13

F IRST THING ON Sunday morning, Jimmy slipped out the front door with his cap pulled down low over his eyes. He passed by the gallows. It hadn't been used for several days, but it was still there, standing silent watch over the people of Thomas Street. The Castle obviously wasn't expecting any surprises during Robert Emmet's trial tomorrow. He glanced at the stage as he ambled past, swearing it looked even bigger than before, and then he turned down Dirty Lane towards the river.

He had wasted the whole day yesterday wondering what to do about Kitty. He'd gone back-and-forth about the whole thing for hours, pacing a new groove in his warped wooden floor. But he wasn't going to waste today. If this trial went as it was looking like it would go, the entire city could explode. He wanted out of Dublin before he got caught up in it. Up to now, he'd been so fixated on the cheap boat from Limerick, and on trying to gather enough funds for two tickets, that he hadn't really considered alternatives. The next Limerick sailing wasn't until some time in November, and he couldn't wait that long. It was time for a new plan. And this time, he had coin. Jimmy pushed away the accompanying guilt; he could worry about that once he was on the boat. Yesterday, he'd been caught up in questions about what he should have done, or what could have happened if he'd been open with Ma, but he wasn't going to let that happen today.

On reaching the Liffey, he laughed as he realized he was *still* trying to convince himself he was doing the right thing. Then he thought of Da, of his excitable talk of building a New Ireland, all while young Jimmy was reeling from the news that his father was heading off to war. He'd been too young back then to question Da's logic, but something struck him now. Wasn't that what his cousin was doing in America, Donal and all other Irish immigrants? Weren't they all diligently building a new Ireland while everyone back home played at soldiers and got killed? Maybe the brave thing to do was to take that same leap, leave it all behind.

Crossing over Essex Bridge, Jimmy felt a touch of nervousness. Gone were the days when someone from The Liberties had to fear for their life when heading over to the Northside, but that gave him little comfort. He hewed to the wall of Ormond Quay, following it straight down towards the new Custom House building that had been erected on an empty plot to the east of the city proper. Boats still left from almost anywhere downstream of where he'd just crossed The Liffey, but all the ticket offices were now concentrated around the wet docks, which had been constructed to the rear of the Custom House, rather than scattered along the quays like before. Jimmy didn't like it, but he didn't have a choice.

He finally found the place, tucked away behind the new docks. He groaned; the queue was out the door and around the corner. He scratched his chin for a moment, resigning himself to his fate and taking his place at the rear of the line. If he wanted to get going this week, this route was his only option. It wasn't ideal; he'd have to go via Liverpool, but he could secure a berth on the transatlantic leg right here, from this office. Ships left for America almost every day. However, the next one sailing direct that still had room wasn't until the following Thursday; it seemed Jimmy wasn't the only one desperate to escape. He tucked his hands into his pockets as he waited. The engorged clouds that had threatened Dublin all morning had moved south towards Wicklow. *That wind is good for something at least,* he thought ruefully.

The fella in front of him finally took the newspaper out from under his arm. The Emmet trial was the big story on the front page. He leaned a little closer to get a proper look.

"Do you mind?"

"Sorry," he mumbled, not realizing he'd been crowding the poor fella.

"No," came the reply, as the man handed Jimmy the newspaper. "Do you mind telling me what it says? I can't get half of what they're talking about."

He took the paper, shuffling it. "I'll do my best." Jimmy scanned the article as a couple of others gathered around. He cleared his throat. "It starts off with a brief mention of the July Rising and Mr. Emmet's salubrious family home."

"How do they describe it exactly?"

"The house?"

"No, the bloody Rising!"

He scanned it again for the actual phrase. "Doomed folly."

The man grunted, which Jimmy took as his cue to continue. "Then there is a short mention of the other men who have been executed." He looked up. "No names, though."

Pushing thoughts of Kitty out of his mind, he continued. "And then, after mentioning that the trial of Mr. Emmet takes place this coming Monday, the writer goes on a bit of a ramble praising the enlightened system of British justice."

That brought more than a few grumbles from the assembled men, which made Jimmy nervous. Expressing seditious attitudes was hardly unknown in Dublin, but the area around Custom House was crawling with soldiers and sailors, as well as the Watch and various brigades of the hated Militia, shipped in from ports all over Ireland. Martial law was still in place, had been since the July Rising, and anyone with half a brain gave the Militia a wide berth. They had gone completely wild in '98, and all sorts of stories abounded about the excesses committed, the atrocities wrought on the Catholics. If even half the stories were true... Jimmy shook his head and returned the newspaper before he was asked to read any more. He pointedly avoided eye contact with the others, who soon shuffled back into line.

Jimmy remembered the night of the Rising. He had been out for a wander, making his way up Francis Street, enjoying a warm, dry evening for once, when he'd bumped into Paulie Grogan. Paulie had acted awful suspicious when Jimmy invited him for a pint.

"I'd say you'd be best staying at home tonight," was all his friend would say, before hurrying off towards The Coombe. He'd laughed it off at the time, but when he turned onto Thomas Street he could tell something was up. Cornmarket House had been taken over by a rowdy group that challenged anyone who ventured past, demanding to know if they were "out"—which meant only one thing. He'd hurried right home to Ma.

She was at the window, fretting—this was before her health took a turn for the worse—and he joined her, watching a procession of torches march down the street. The first shots rang out shortly afterwards, and he had ordered Ma away from the window. Ma followed his advice meekly, taking to the bed with a troubled look on her brow, only coming back to life when he'd made for the door. She had reacted hysterically, he remembered, to his suggestion of going downstairs to see what was going on. It had taken him ten minutes to calm her down so he could explain he only meant calling in to the neighbors below to see what was happening. Even so, she made him swear he'd come right back. Thankfully, they had carted away the dead before Ma had dared to peek out the window once more. She'd been ashen-faced at the smoke rising over the city, the British troops stomping up and down the streets, the cries of neighbors being hauled away to Kilmainham Gaol for questioning.

When Jimmy eventually did make it outside the building, he couldn't make head nor tail of what was going on. One fella claimed it had been little more than a drunken riot; several others disagreed, saying they'd seen United men with pikes coming within a hair's breadth of the Castle. One drunkard even said that the whole thing had been called off at the last moment, and the only clashes had been to cover the retreat of the main body of rebels, who had now melted into the countryside, ready to strike again once the French landed. One thing was clear, though: Major Sirr was on the warpath. He was determined to see the rebels, and particularly their leader, hang. Thomas Street had been surrounded. The army took over the Cornmarket Building at the top of the street, and the Militia guarded the archway of St. James' Gate at the beginning. And it seemed like every side street and alleyway leading in was crawling with patrols. Even the bridges across the Liffey had a permanent guard, and anyone crossing was questioned.

It was a mess. And all for nothing. The rebels failed, the French never came good on their promises, and Robert Emmet was captured. Jimmy wondered if Napoleon had ever intended to invade Ireland, or whether it was all a smokescreen intended to distract the

British with a rebellion at home while he snatched the rest of Europe. These thoughts occupied Jimmy for the next three hours while he queued, but he finally got his hands on the ticket—a pretty grand term for a wispy slip of paper. He'd expected something more substantial in exchange for the five guineas he counted out on that man's table. But with the prize safely ensconced in his money belt, Jimmy began the long walk back along the Liffey to the first bridge across to the Southside, just opposite Capel Street. It was interesting, seeing the city from this side of the water. The hopeless tangle of roads, laneways and quays had a little more logic to it from here—once you thought of the river itself as the main road into Dublin. For a moment, he lost himself in the beauty of ships lining the quay, the swarms of porters racing to and fro, the strong breeze tugging at furled sails, masts waving gently as the vessels bobbed in the tidal river.

And then the wind changed direction; he wrinkled his nose and hurried to the bridge.

14

RAIN BATTERED THE sole window in Jimmy's cramped garret, making him wish it were Friday instead of Monday, so he could depart without further delay. As if steeling himself, he added the weather to the list of things he wouldn't miss. He immediately felt guilty, thinking of Ma buried in the hard ground of Bully's Acre, so he tried to focus on anything else—the *bodhrán* beat of raindrops on the windowpane, or the citizens on the street below, hurrying from one awning to the next.

Jimmy exhaled, only then realizing he had been holding his breath. He had made another too. He had to at least try speaking with Kitty one last time, knowing he'd regret it forever otherwise. But how could he find her? The crowd across the river would give him little joy if he went wandering around Smithfield asking questions. Which left Mahaffy.

Figuring there was little point showing up at The

White Bull before lunchtime, Jimmy busied himself with practicalities. He was supposed to inform the landlord he was leaving, but wondered if he should bother. Rent was due each Friday, but he was paid up, so he could just leave. The landlord would figure it out soon enough, and Jimmy hardly owed that cur a favor. He'd need to get all of Ma's things over to Nora's beforehand, though, or else everything would be turfed out on the street—anything that crook landlord couldn't sell, at least. And he had to speak with his aunt, of course, but not until closer to his departure. He didn't want several days of goodbyes. She might try talking him out of it, despite what she had said, and he didn't need his resolve tested; he was already doubting himself enough as it was.

Friday. It was only four days away. Then he was gone, forever. He looked around at all the rubbish that had piled up in the room over the years, still wishing he could leave tomorrow. All of the objects were like little weights attached to him, harmless on their own but collectively pinning him to the ground.

He jumped into action, piling all of Ma's old clothes on the bed alongside a smaller pile of his own clothes. It didn't take long. He had only what he was wearing, another fresh shirt, and some spare smallclothes. Nonetheless, he took stock of it all. Various herbs and whatnot in jars and tins he piled on the table. Nora might make use of them, if she could decipher their contents. Sadly, the recipe for Ma's magic tincture had died with her, but maybe Nora could get one of the kids to replicate it. *Someone will make money off that one day*, he told himself.

Under Ma's bed, behind the straw mattress he used to sleep on, he found a small wooden box. He pulled it out and blew a thick layer of dust from the lid. The sides of the box were plain, but the lid was embossed with a fantastical beast that appeared to be breathing fire. He stared at the engraving for a moment before flipping the box open.

On the top was a lock of hair, presumably his own, judging by the color. Beside it was his mother's wedding ring. She had stopped wearing it about a year after Da was killed. Ma never said why, but Jimmy assumed she wanted one less reminder in a city filled with ghosts. He held it up, reading the date engraved on the inside. It was well after the year Ma had told him she married Da. Mahaffy had been telling the truth, he noted. The ring fit snugly on his little finger. Underneath, at the bottom of the box, was a tattered, yellowing sheaf of paper. He unfolded it carefully, his pulse quickening as he realized what it was: a map of The Colonies.

His father had bought it off a destitute ship's captain and given it to Jimmy when he was just a pup. He remembered how Ma used to give out to him when she caught him staring it. Da had nailed it to the wall across from where he slept, in their old room downstairs on the ground floor. Jimmy had always wondered what happened to it. The map had simply disappeared one day, right around the time they found out Da wasn't coming home, he realized. Jimmy folded it out on the floor, blowing the dust away to get a better look. His eyes sailed down the coast, imagining the first ships charting this territory, gazing out at places that would come to be named Virginia, New Jersey, and Maryland.

"See you soon," he said, tapping it gently before folding it away.

Outside, the bell tolled for noon. Time to corner Kitty's uncle.

Despite counseling himself to remain cool and collected, Jimmy raced down the two flights of stairs and out the door, only slowing when he reached the entrance to the pub. Inside The White Bull, he eyeballed the barman. "I need Mahaffy," he demanded.

"Who's asking?"

Biting back a smart response, he simply said, "Jimmy O'Flaherty."

The barman ducked into the back, returning less than a minute later only to completely ignore Jimmy, casually wiping the counter as if he wasn't there.

"Well?" he demanded, stepping into the barman's eye line.

"He told you to fuck off."

Jimmy was caught off guard for a moment. *Kitty must have told him what I said on the way home from the countryside,* he realized. He gulped. That confirmed Mahaffy was involved somehow. "Tell him it's about Kitty," he said, trying to keep his voice even, despite his gritted teeth.

The barman stared him down for a moment, as if contemplating whether to bother his arse, but disappeared once more. He didn't reappear for another couple of minutes. When he did, he beckoned Jimmy closer. "When you leave, use the side door."

Nodding, Jimmy went around the bar and through to the backroom.

Mahaffy looked haggard, Jimmy noted as he crossed the space in front of his table. "I don't want to waste your time," he said. "I'm looking for Kitty."

"Why?"

Jimmy had to struggle to remain calm. "I need to speak with her," he said.

"What about?"

"I just want to talk to her." They stared at each other for a minute, but Jimmy broke eye contact first. "I'm leaving," he said. "The ticket is bought and all. I'll be gone in a few days—forever." He looked up hopefully. "I just want to say goodbye."

Mahaffy yawned. "Sorry." He rubbed his face, which brought a little color back to his cheeks but did nothing for the dark circles under his eyes. "The last few days have been hectic."

"So I heard."

"Anyone mention the cause of it?" Mahaffy eyed him curiously.

"Sure, I was away. But I heard it was July all over again. Doors kicked in. Fellas hauled off. Didn't hear the reason, though."

"I'll tell you." He leaned in menacingly. "Someone talked when they shouldn't have."

Jimmy tried to hold Mahaffy's mad stare, his heart beating so terribly he worried his teeth would rattle. "You know me," he replied. "Never was much for talking."

Mahaffy slowly eased himself back into his chair, before nodding. "Good." He finally dropped his stare, scratching his chin.

"About Kitty…"

"I'm looking for her myself," Mahaffy blurted out.

That surprised him, but he tried to keep it from his face.

"I'm a little worried about her, truth be told. I've been trying to talk sense to her, but she's too bloody stubborn. Just like her mother was, God rest her soul."

"What's the matter?"

Mahaffy chose his words carefully. "There's too much trouble in Dublin right now. I'd… prefer she spent some time with my sister down in Wicklow." He paused. "Out of harm's way."

Jimmy's throat tightened. "And she's refusing?"

"You know what she's like." He snorted. "She was even talking about going up to the Castle and demanding Anne Devlin's release." Mahaffy reached across the table. "We have to stop her. If she's recognized…"

"I'll find her." Jimmy stood.

"I don't know where she's staying, before you ask. We had a house she used in Smithfield, but we have to avoid that for now." His eyes widened a touch. "But I know where she'll be tomorrow."

Jimmy nodded, realizing with bitter irony that the gallows' work would soon be done. "I'll find her," he promised, before turning on his heel and marching out the door. What he didn't tell Mahaffy was that he suspected where Kitty might be this evening too. Emmet's trial might be a foregone conclusion, but the Castle was sure to drag it out for the whole day to show the world just how fair they were being.

He kept up a good clip the whole way down Thomas Street, ignoring calls from the traders at Cornmarket and continuing on past Christchurch to the gates of Dublin Castle, glad to find that Kitty hadn't been foolish enough to harangue the guards about the fate of Anne Devlin. With a sigh of relief, he turned down Parliament Street toward the river, passing the fancy shops with their lead-glass windows and gazing with envy at the books inside. The centerpiece of the display was a thoroughly ostentatious edition featuring hand-painted illustrations and gilt-edged pages. The tome looked so heavy that he wondered how anyone held it comfortably. The intended audience was probably those gentlemen who preferred announcing what they had read, he supposed, to the actual act of reading.

Copper Alley cut across Parliament Street about halfway down, providing a humorously salacious interlude between the snooty shopfronts with their expensive oil lamps and fastidious window arrangements and haughty proprietors. A drunkard stumbled across the street, followed by a prostitute complaining he'd welched on his bill. The ladies in their finery clutched at pearls and adjusted shawls, more offended by the harlot's lack of shame than anything. The men tutted and made threatening noises about lodging official complaints, while running their eyes over the prostitute's body and, no doubt, wondering how much she charged.

The gentle slope of the street ended at the Liffey, where all classes of men united to pinch noses. Today, the stench was particularly bad. A low tide and a dry spell had combined to expose the seaweed-covered rocks on either side of the river, which was now reduced to a deeper channel running through the center. Without the water's protection, the rocks bore the brunt of the overhanging privies along the riverside. There was talk of clearing all buildings off the quays and opening the river up to the public, but Jimmy was sure they'd make a balls of it, if they ever got around to it. A westerly breeze meant the odor had nowhere to escape to, either. Its fetor hung over the riverbank like a deadly cloud.

And, just then, the heavens opened.

Rain lashed down at a hellish rate, as if trying to make up for the last few dry days. A fella carrying a door almost knocked him off the footpath, and Jimmy cursed as he watched him stagger away under the weight of the thing, envious of his protection from the elements. He took shelter in a shopfront, beside a young boy with sodden broadsheets curling around his arm.

"Is the trial still going?" Jimmy asked, taking off his cap for a moment.

The boy nodded vigorously.

"Where is it being held?"

The little peddler pointed across the river in response, and Jimmy realized the poor tyke was mute.

Essex Bridge was thick with people. Militiamen had set up in the middle, questioning anyone crossing over to the Northside. Best to keep going down beyond Wood Quay, he decided, to see if Ormond Bridge was any better. A whistle sounded. Glancing back over his shoulder, he saw two men on horseback attempting to clear the bridge. Whatever was going on back there, he was better off out of it. People didn't need much provocation at the moment. Soldiers in particular.

Jimmy pressed on and a passerby confirmed it was the Green Street Courthouse he was looking for, and that proceedings looked like they would continue for some time. Given Kitty's interest in the executions, it was a fair guess she might show up at the trial. And if the action back there was anything to go by, she wouldn't be the only person in Dublin with that notion.

Luckily, Ormond Bridge was quieter. Staring up at the impressive new Four Courts building facing the water, he cursed the fact that he was heading elsewhere, deeper into the Northside. He also realized he was more scared of crossing The Liffey than traversing the Atlantic. Reminding himself that there was no sign hanging around his neck identifying him as being from The Liberties, he straightened his back, puffed out his chest, and walked up Charles Street as if he'd done it a thousand times.

There was no need to ask for directions. As soon as he reached the corner of Pill Lane it was clear everyone was heading the same way. Some were holding candles. Others were crying, as if their son were in the dock, rather than a stranger's. Still, he allowed, they had probably suffered tragedies of their own. Pockets of rowdiness spilled out too, groups piling out of the pubs and taverns that lined every street leading to The Liffey, but overall, a solemn tone ruled... until they got to Green Street, where an edgy crowd surrounded the courthouse.

Jimmy ran his hands through his hair. He'd been hoping Kitty would be easy to spot, one of a few dedicated enough to come down here for a blow-by-blow account of the trial, but the street was jammed. He stepped up onto a window-ledge for a better view, hanging out of the iron bars that protected the glass. A group of redcoats blocked off the north end of Green Street, no doubt to keep the route clear for any reinforcements coming in from the Royal Barracks next to Oxmantown Green. Was it disorder the British feared most, he wondered, or a rescue attempt? The crowd was drunk on talk that Michael Dwyer planned a daring escape for Emmet, that he'd secretly left his mountain stronghold last week and infiltrated the city with a select group of men, all ready to strike.

The soldiers guarding the entrance didn't seem convinced; he saw one even stifle a yawn. Access to the courthouse was controlled by just two men, although those outside weren't clamoring to enter, instead content to wait and feed off the scraps of information making their way from the courtroom. He searched all the faces, but Kitty's was nowhere to be seen. So he waited. Climbing the ledge again a little later, he noticed that the company of soldiers to the north had moved a good deal closer. A second had joined them on the southern end of the street, their intimidating presence undercut by bored expressions and weapons dangling by their sides. Nevertheless, Jimmy took it as his cue to leave.

15

THERE WAS BUT a small knot of people outside Kilmainham Gaol, and Jimmy could immediately see that Kitty wasn't one of them. Unsure of his next step, he stared up at the jail, its facade cold and unyielding in the morning sun. The gray limestone walls were said to be four feet thick in places, but the damp still crept into the cells. His skin crawled as he imagined the hundreds of inmates wasting away in the dark, many guilty of little more than being in the wrong place when the order came down to fill the prisons.

At London's urging, the Castle had thousands arrested after July's failed rebellion. Fellas were locked up for weeks, and then released without being questioned. It was mad. Some were rebels, to be sure, but most just happened to cross paths with the roving groups of Militiamen that swarmed over the capital for much of August. The idea was to intimidate, to paralyze. Officially, the hunt was on for the rebel leader, Robert

Emmet, and any seditious elements collaborating with foreign spies. But it was clear the real intent was to mark everyone's card, to show that British power had no limits. And that there was nothing Napoleon Bonaparte or the United Irishmen could do about that.

He wondered about those still trapped inside. Would they ever be released, and what shape would they be when they were? Fellas lost their minds in there. Stories abounded; he didn't doubt them either. He couldn't imagine being caged up like that, with no idea if you'd ever be let go. Some never made it out at all, of course. People just disappeared. Fell through the cracks of the system and were forgotten. Like poor Anne Devlin. Jimmy blessed himself, even though he couldn't remember the last time he had prayed properly.

That mute boy was making his rounds, trying to flog his last few copies. *Leftovers from yesterday*, Jimmy thought, until a quick glance proved otherwise. "EMMET TO HANG," screamed the headline. But the smaller words underneath really piqued his interest: "Jilted Rebel Leader Blasts Napoleon."

He scanned the text for any reference to the promised invasion fleet. Apparently, Emmet had given quite a moving speech from the dock after his death sentence had been handed down. In the dock, before Judge

Norbury handed down the death sentence, Emmet had blamed the French for not backing his plot and made some very strong statements about fighting them on the beaches and burning their boats.

"This is horseshit," someone spat beside him. "Are you reading this?"

Jimmy turned and gave a quick nod to a fella who was working himself up into an awful lather. "Where's that little bastard gone?"

"What do you want with him?" Jimmy said, hoping to stall him until he'd cooled down.

He scrunched up the broadsheet. "It's lies. All lies." He blinked up at the sky. "The bastards." He sighed. "We'll never get a moment's peace from their machinations. After '98, I thought I'd seen it all: half-hangings, pitch-cappings, torching farms, attacking families, slaughtering women and children for no godly reason. But this is another level. They must have planted this bit here." He tapped the page. "Robert Emmet never said that. The fuckers. They knew this'd make its way to Paris quick smart. The Castle must have planted this story."

Jimmy couldn't help himself. "How do you know?"

"I was fucking there. He never said that." His face was so red he looked fit to burst. "Where is that little shit?"

"Come on, now. It's not his fault."

The fella looked like he was about to smack Jimmy for a second, but he calmed somewhat. "I know, sorry. It's just… if you'd heard that speech. It's a sin to desecrate a man's memory like that."

"He's not dead yet," someone else spoke up from behind.

"Aye," agreed others.

The fella turned to them. "Keating, do you have the other one? The real speech." He returned to Jimmy, jabbing his finger at the headline: "LET NO MAN WRITE MY EPITAPH."

A lump formed in Jimmy's throat as he began to read.

He was surprised Emmet could muster up such coherence after twelve hours on his feet chained to the dock, let alone genuine eloquence. Especially with that bastard Judge Norbury attempting to shout him down any time he got going. But Emmet was like a torrent. It seemed he had been quiet all day, confusing observers, offering no defense to the charges laid against him, and calling no witnesses on his behalf. Instead, the rebel leader opted to finally unburden his thoughts when afforded the opportunity to speak before being sentenced. His speech went on for ten minutes or more before Judge Norbury finally silenced him and pronounced the death sentence.

And the fella was right. Robert Emmet's only negative comments about the French regarded the possibility of them landing as invaders, rather than allies of the United Irishmen. The differences were subtle, but enough. Jimmy shook his head. The deviousness of the English knew no bounds.

The church bells chimed once. An hour after noon, and still Emmet hadn't left Kilmainham Gaol. The fellas around him explained that the British wanted to drag out Emmet's torment. Rather than send him straight to Thomas Street, they planned to parade him around the city first. His carriage would go north through Islandbridge and across the river before turning down Barrack Street, running through Smithfield, and then, eventually, crossing at Queen's Bridge and making its way up Bridgefoot Street. Jimmy figured it would take them an hour or more, and that route was simply too long to search for Kitty. Besides, there was only one place she was going to be when Emmet climbed the scaffold.

St. Catherine's Church.

16

TENS OF THOUSANDS of souls crammed into Thomas Street and the surrounding laneways, a great seething, angry mass of Dubliners. Jimmy shoved his way to the front, knowing that if Kitty turned up anywhere, it would be there. He immediately regretted that decision when faced with a wall of bayonets. He dug his heels in, but those behind kept pushing him forward. All the soldiers had to do was keep their blades pointed at chest-level and the front line of the crowd did their work for them—desperately holding back the rest so they wouldn't be impaled by English steel.

Jimmy wormed his way back a couple of rows in retreat from the blades. From here, he could get a proper look at the scaffold looming above him so ominously. A single rope swung there this morning, hovering over the bench Emmet would stand on to reach the noose. But there was a new addition to proceedings: a butcher's block to the right of the scaffold was the center of much speculation. High Treason convictions carried the sentence of being hung, drawn, and quartered, but the latter two were rarely carried out. Today, it looked like the Crown was sticking to the letter of the law, even despite the huge crowd—or because of it, perhaps.

A great rolling wail started somewhere well behind him, heralding the arrival of the prisoner, Jimmy guessed. He moved quickly. Taking advantage of the chaos as the throng surged forward, he wrestled his way through the mob. If Kitty wasn't at the front near the stage, perhaps she was to the right, where Robert Emmet was now arriving from Kilmainham Gaol. He fought his way through until he could see the gilded carriage, strangely out of place when a simple cart had sufficed for the other unfortunates. But the Castle was putting on a show.

His eyes swept the crowd, searching for Kitty, as he leaned all his weight back onto those shoving from behind. A soldier approached the carriage and opened the door. A weak-looking man stepped out—Emmet, he guessed, based on the newspaper sketches, although they seemed to have exaggerated his features. In the flesh, his face was less angular, his nose less pointed. His eyes, far from being beady, burned with a fierce passion that belied his poor physical state. His skin was so pale it was almost translucent, and his black coat hung loosely on his slight frame. Yet for all that, Jimmy thought he appeared unbroken. If he were to judge men by their countenances alone, Jimmy thought the accompanying vicar looked more disturbed than the condemned Emmet. Some kind of argument ensued between Emmet and his captors, which increased the agitation of the vicar. Eventually, he turned to the crowd. Briefly, the mask slipped, and in place of a feared rebel leader, Jimmy saw Robert Emmet for who he truly was: a scared man, not much older than himself, facing death.

In a flash, Emmet regained his composure. He stepped towards the crowd, his face animated again. "My friends," he said, speaking loudly and quickly before the guards could silence him. "I die in peace and with sentiments of universal love and kindness towards all men." He was hustled towards the scaffold before he could speak further, and the crowd surged towards the stage, giving Jimmy little space to breathe, let alone to hunt for Kitty, who was still nowhere to be seen.

The rebel commander climbed the stage and removed his watch, handing it to the executioner. Jimmy, still caught in the crush, almost tripped over a discarded box that had probably been abandoned by a ballad singer. It was solid enough to support his weight, but as soon as he mounted it, a soldier roared in his direction; Jimmy pretended not to hear.

From this vantage point, he could see over most of the crowd, all watching in open-mouthed horror as Emmet's hands were bound behind his back. It made him dizzy, all these people in one place. But at that moment he saw her. At least he thought it was her. A face had flashed towards him for an instant; green eyes. It could have been her. He waited for a moment, trying to spot her again, still ignoring the soldier's remonstrations. It was no use; he couldn't pick her out.

Desperate now, he jumped down and forced his way back through the other side—a task that was a little easier now that he was moving in the same direction as everyone else. Maddeningly, he still couldn't see Kitty anywhere. A sudden calm fell over the crowd. Jimmy glanced back up to see that Emmet was being ushered to the hanging bench.

"Speech!" went up a cry from the back, its fervor matched by hundreds more voices calling in unison, then thousands. Jimmy noticed a slight smile twitch Emmet's lip as the executioner, bearing the black hood, approached. As Tom Galvin held the hood aloft to place it over the condemned man's head, a thunder of hooves rocked the scaffold. The crowd turned as one toward the sound, hungry for the dramatic rescue they had prayed for all day—everyone except Jimmy, that is. He kept his eyes fixed on Emmet. The man's stoic demeanor betrayed him for one cruel moment. Hope flickered across his features. But it was just a company of English dragoons, eager to witness his death.

The hangman hooded him and led Emmet to the bench underneath the scaffold. He helped him up onto the bench and guided his head into the noose, which was black and greasy from so much use; they hadn't even bothered to change the rope. Proceedings were strangely civil, though. Emmet's hands were bound behind his back, the executioner even checking that the bindings were not too tight. The mob ceased surging forwards, the assembly collectively holding its breath. Jimmy took advantage of the lull to slip through to the front once more. Even the bayonet-wielding soldiers were casting glances behind them to the bench. The prisoner shuffled his feet on the wooden stage. The executioner leaned in.

"Are you ready?" Jimmy could hear him ask, but the condemned man only responded with a shake of his hooded head.

Tom Galvin gave him a moment, wiping the sweat from his brow as he eyed the butcher's block at center stage. He turned back to Emmet once more. "Are you ready now?" he asked.

"Not yet," was the reply.

The executioner turned away to exchange words with an officer, out of earshot.

A spell had been cast over Thomas Street, slowing time and calming a once-seething crowd, at least momentarily.

For a third time, the hangman leaned in.

This time, Emmet's reply was louder than before. "No!" he cried, but the executioner had already given him a shove.

He dangled from the neck, his legs jerking and kicking against the air like an upturned calf, and wrenched his hands free from the bindings, his fingers grasping at the dirty rope that choked his throat. The crowd fell silent. Jimmy was glad he couldn't see the poor man's face.

A surge came from behind, with much greater force than before. Jimmy was almost knocked from his feet, only managing to stay upright by grabbing onto the fella beside him. The act nearly dragged the pair of them to the cobblestones, until a heave from the other direction straightened them again. He shifted his stance, securing his footing, and then searched for Kitty once more. An officer approached the gallows, his squinting eyes assessing the hangman's work with approval. He turned and said something to the executioner, and a brief argument ensued before the officer gave his orders. The hangman folded his arms, sneering out at the crowd, absorbing all their hate. Two soldiers climbed the stage and approached the scaffold. They let the slack out of the rope, and Robert Emmet's body fell to the stage. The crowd gasped and then fell silent, fearing what must follow.

A group of soldiers detached from the wall of men fronting the stage and marched to surround a cart that had pulled up on the left-hand side. *For the remains*, Jimmy guessed. But instead of tossing the corpse in, a pair of soldiers dragged it to the butcher's block, like two sheepish friends dragging home a drunkard.

Robert Emmet looked like a reluctant penitent when they kneeled his still warm body before the butcher's block. The hangman unfolded his thick arms and reached behind the stage to produce a long butcher's knife. He looked nervous, for once, as he approached the corpse, as if Emmet were a prize pig waiting to be gutted for the King. The blade glinted in the sun as the executioner told the two soldiers to fuck off.

Then he started cutting.

The crowd snapped from its stupor. It pressed forward again, roaring and wailing, the people not quite believing what they were seeing. Jimmy stared slack-jawed in shock himself. Rumors had abounded that Judge Norbury had directed the beheading to take place, but most had shrugged it off as political theater. Not now. The executioner hacked and sawed, as blood—so much blood—sprayed the air and ran in a steady trickle down the butcher's block, off the front of the stage, and onto the cobbles of Thomas Street. A feral dog squeezed up between the assembled ankles to lap up the rebel leader's blood, snarling when someone tried to shoo him away.

Jimmy wanted to avert his eyes, but he was trans-fixed, realizing with horror that the spurting arc of arterial blood meant that Emmet must be alive. Sweat poured from the hangman's brow as he continued to hack and saw through sinew and tendon. Even a spray of blood that caught him in the face didn't halt the executioner's grim work. Several grisly minutes later, he conceded defeat and switched to the axe. Eventually, he hacked the head free, the body slumping unceremonious-ly to the stage.

The hangman stared out at the crowd, his eyes un-readable as he picked up Emmet's severed head by the hair. He walked to the right-hand side of the stage and held it aloft.

"This is the head of a traitor!" he boomed. "This is the head of Robert Emmet."

Jimmy glanced at the faces around him, open-mouthed in disbelief. The executioner stood holding the head for a moment—glaring out at the crowd as blood continued to drip down onto the stage beneath. Then he marched over to the left-hand side of the stage. "This is the head of a traitor!" he roared. "This is the head of Robert Emmet."

The head made an empty thud on the bloodied wooden boards as he let it slip from his grasp. Jimmy couldn't see what happened next. He was knocked right off his feet, trampled by a furious, howling crowd seeking its revenge. He managed to prop himself up on one elbow, only to be shoved down once more, his mouth flooded with the coppery taste of blood. He pulled his knees into his chest and rolled onto his side, cradling his head in his hands, waiting for the storm to pass over him.

Overhead, shots rang out, and the rancor of the mob seemed to abate. He stumbled onto his knees, then grappled his way to his feet. *Kitty.* For one brief moment she was there. Then she disappeared back into a crushing swarm of faces, all of which suddenly screamed as they collapsed, crumbling headfirst into the ground. Like a madman, he tore through the crowd, elbowing, kicking, scratching his way to the pile of stricken bodies. He wrenched others out of the way until he found her, battered, bloodied, and unconscious. Someone shoved him in the back as he cleared the space to pick her up, and he wheeled around and clocked the fella square in the jaw, sending him toppling backwards.

A crack on the back of the head sent dark spots fizzing before his eyes, and a dull ache spread across his crown. Mustering all his strength, he scooped Kitty up off the cobbles and turned to face his assailant. "Back off!" he roared, scarlet streaming down his face. "Or, by God, I'll kill you dead."

The group facing him reeled back, first in fear and then in sympathy when they saw him cradling an injured girl. Jimmy forced his way clear of the riot. He marched down Thomas Street away from the tumult, holding Kitty aloft like a macabre trophy—as if she was somehow proof of his most fervent belief: that it's the innocent who suffer most from all this madness.

17

MERCIFULLY, THE FRONT door of his building was ajar, so he didn't have to set Kitty down to enter. Instead, he carried her all the way to the top floor and kicked his own door open while still holding her. Gently, he placed her in Ma's bed, her blood staining the fresh bedsheets crimson. After pouring a jug of stale water over his filthy hands, he checked her wounds. They seemed superficial, although there was some nasty swelling on the back of her head. Out in the street below, the madness continued, preventing any chance of getting a medic.

Taking a damp cloth, he tenderly washed the blood from her face and checked her arms and legs for any breakages. Most of the blood ran from a single cut on her lip, he noted with relief. After making her as comfortable as he could, he brought a chair to the bedside, so he could watch over her. Then Jimmy O'Flaherty prayed, for the first time in years.

A low, keening moan coming from the bed woke him.

Kitty.

He leaped up and leaned over her. "I'm here," he said in a soothing tone, patting the damp cloth against her forehead. "Look at the state of you."

"Where am I?" She was still groggy, but now cogent.

Jimmy smiled in relief.

"Ah, for feck's sake," she said when her eyes focused.

"Hello, Kitty."

"What happened?" She tried rise but fell back, dizzy.

"Best take it slowly," he cautioned. "Must have gotten some bump on that head. You were out cold for hours."

"I remember falling…"

Jimmy nodded.

She put her hand to her lip. "It hurts."

"I'll give you something for the pain in a minute." He tried to remember where he had packed Ma's *poitín*. "Just take it easy."

After locating the bottle of firewater, he poured a little onto a clean handkerchief. "Stay still now," he warned, dabbing her swollen lip.

The barest touch of it made her yelp.

"Sorry, but if it stings that means it's working."

Kitty raised an eyebrow. "Your mother told you that too?"

Jimmy laughed. "Da, actually."

"Give me that bottle." She propped herself up on her elbows.

When he handed it over, she took a swig.

"Easy now," he said, snatching it back.

Kitty let herself fall back onto the bed, wincing again when her head hit the pillow.

"You don't look too good yourself," she said, some life coming back into her green eyes.

He looked at the bottle. "Only a couple of smacks," he said, taking a sip. "It got a bit wild back there."

She reached for his arm and squeezed. "Thank you. It was horrible." Her eyes pooled with tears. "All of it."

"Aye, it was."

"Give me that *poitín*." Kitty sat up again. "My father used to make his own, before…"

Jimmy realized she'd never spoken of her parents. She passed the bottle back, her cheeks flushed with a sudden vigor, and he allowed the silence to fill the room.

"You saved me, so you deserve the truth, or as much of it as I can tell." Her eyes hardened. "If you breathe a word of this to my uncle, I won't have to come after you, because he'll put you in the ground himself."

"Sure who would I tell?" Jimmy could see his reply didn't satisfy her, so he swore an oath on his mother's grave.

Eventually, she began. "That man you saw me with, he was a spy. He sold information to the Castle, which cost us five good men. I didn't kill him, but I led him to his death. And I'm not sorry either."

"So that show you put on in the pub...?"

"An act. Yes." Her eyes flashed. "I'm no whore."

Jimmy breathed a sigh of relief, but her revelation didn't alleviate all of his concerns. Kitty had helped murder a man—spy or no. He watched her, his heart heavy. "What kind of mess does Mahaffy have you involved in?"

"I make my own decisions," she snapped.

"I just meant—"

"If you think I'm some kind of naïve girl who's gotten mixed up in something she doesn't understand, then think again. I knew exactly what I was doing, and nobody forced me to do anything. And I don't need saving by you or anyone else."

"But... why?"

She eyed the bottle of *poitín* and then took a deep breath. "I grew up in Wicklow," she said, "not too far from Baltinglass—about five miles from Maeve's farm. I had a happy childhood. Life was hard at times, but I had a mother and father who loved me and two older brothers—fiercely protective, of course." She paused.

"And then the Militia took it all away." She took a drink, and Jimmy wasn't sure whether it was the *poitín* or the memory that made her shudder. "I never believed the Devil was real until he loomed over me. I'll never forget those cold, lifeless eyes. Priests say the soul is the spark that gives life to the body, but that man had no soul. None at all. Hepenstall was his name, Lieutenant Edward Hepenstall of the Wicklow Militia."

A lump clotted in Jimmy's throat. He recognized the name; any Catholic would.

"The Walking Gallows himself." She stared up at the ceiling. "There was no warning. They simply rode into the farm one day, ordered us all out into the yard, lined us up against the wall of the farmhouse, oldest to youngest. Hepenstall was in command—a giant of a man, six-and-a-half feet if he was an inch, broad shouldered too, not wiry at all. Big hands on him like a pair of shovels, yet soft-looking like a gentleman. But there was nothing soft about him. He walked up the line, staring each of us in the face, wrinkling his nose like we were filthy animals. When he reached my father, he stopped."

Kitty stared at her hands, knotted together in her lap, as if drawing the strength to continue. She did eventually, after a deep breath. "Hepenstall pointed at my father and claimed to have information that he was hiding a rebel. It was all lies, of course. My father never had anything to do with the rebels, and my brothers were only interested in chasing girls or hurling. Da explained all this. He insisted there must be some mistake. Hepenstall listened patiently and then said, 'If you won't tell me who the rebel is, I shall have to decide for myself.'"

"We all watched in shock as he started to pace again. He stopped in front of my oldest brother, Mick, and sized him up for a moment. Then he moved onto Colm. He was only two years older than I was, just fifteen. But he pointed at Colm and said, 'This one.'"

"Ma cried out, but two soldiers were on top of her straightaway, holding her down. Another put a blade to my father's throat, daring him to react. 'Where are you taking my son?' Ma screamed. And I'll never forget what Hepenstall did next. It still chills me to the bone. 'We're not taking him anywhere,' he said, and he was smiling— smiling as he said it. 'Fetch the rope. We'll hang him right here.'"

"Mick lunged for Hepenstall, but one of the soldiers

was quicker, and his guts got the butt of a rifle. 'You can't do this,' my father cried.

"But Hepenstall just smiled and said, 'Then tell me who the traitor is.'

"Mick was only just after getting up of the ground, and his blood was up. 'I am,' he said, calm as anything. My poor dad couldn't take this any longer. Looking Hepenstall square in the eye, he said, 'I'm the rebel. Don't listen to them. I took the oath. It's me. I'll make a full confession now. I'll sign anything you want. Just spare my sons, please, I beg you.'

"Hepenstall just laughed again. He turned to his men. 'I make that three confessions, boys.' He leered at my mother. 'Get the rope. We'll hang them all right here.'

"In desperation, Ma wriggled free from the soldiers' grip and flew at Hepenstall like a banshee, scratching wildly at his face. She disappeared under their hail of punches and slumped to the ground. A small mercy that she was unconscious for what happened next."

Jimmy swallowed hard, and she handed him the bottle. "Drink," she ordered. "You'll need it." He took a hearty gulp and handed it back to her while she continued. "I remember Da looking at me and telling me not to be scared. But that only made Hepenstall's twisted smile grow wider. The bastard was enjoying every minute of it."

Kitty took a long swig and cocked her head right back, letting the firewater burn all the way down her throat. "I'm sorry, I've never told anyone—no one except my uncle, all those years ago." Her lips trembled, as if she might break down, but she somehow kept her tears in check.

"There was an argument between Hepenstall and one of his men. I thought someone was trying to rein him in, but it wasn't that at all. This soldier had forgotten the rope. Hepenstall was so enraged, he struck him to the ground with one blow. The sound of that man's jaw cracking was sickening. Then he leaned over, as if to throttle him, but removed his cravat instead.

"Hepenstall stretched the cravat out between his hands, rolling the ends around his fists. 'This will do,' he said, pointing at poor Colm. 'Him first.' Before we even knew what was happening, two of the Militiamen grabbed my brother and dragged him to Hepenstall. He… he looped the cravat around Colm's neck and tied a firm knot around his throat."

Kitty buried her face in her hands. "I didn't even lift a finger. I don't think I even cried out. I was frozen to the spot. I couldn't believe what was happening."

Her voice shook again at the recollection. "Hepenstall stared right at me as he yanked Colm to his feet. Then he turned on his heel, hoisted my brother onto his back like a sick foal, and marched up and down the farmyard while Colm wriggled and kicked and slowly choked to death. Then he did the same to Mick. And then my father."

"Oh, Kitty…"

"When he was done, he threw my Da's body to the dirt like it was nothing at all. My father was a big man, but I don't think Hepenstall even broke a sweat. Then he turned to his men and told them, 'Torch the buildings.'

"'What about the girl?' one asked. At that point, I was hoping he'd kill me too. Praying, even. But he just squinted at me with those lifeless eyes and smiled once more. 'Let her watch,' he said, 'and let her learn.'

"So, no," Kitty said. "I don't feel any guilt over that man's death." Her eyes flashed. "I'd kill them all in their sleep if I could. Slit their throats and let them bleed out like pigs."

Jimmy was lost for words. He accepted the drink from her again in silence. His eyes watered, but he wasn't sure it was from the burn. After giving her back the bottle, he strode to the window. That damned scaffold was still there. He could see a charwoman scrubbing the cobbles at its base. *Robert Emmet's blood.*

Clenching his fists, he turned back Kitty. She looked so fragile, lying there on the bed with her swollen lip, cradling the bottle of *poitín* like a newborn. She was tougher than she looked, but he wanted more than anything to take her away from all of this. He couldn't rid her of her pain, but maybe he could take her to a place where she wasn't surrounded by constant reminders of that terrible day.

Kitty threw off the blanket and carefully swung her legs over the side of the bed.

"Careful," he warned.

She nodded. "Take me to the window," she insisted, as she unsteadily got to her feet.

He rushed to her side, worried she might faint.

"I could do with some air, but I'm not keen on tackling those stairs just yet." Kitty leaned against the window frame, letting the gentle breeze wash over her wan face. She closed her eyes, and Jimmy couldn't help staring, drinking in her beauty.

"You can stay as long as you like."

Her eyes flicked open and some color returned to her cheeks. "That's a most improper proposal, Mr. O'Flaherty."

"I didn't mean—"

He was interrupted by a kiss.

"Ow," she said, pulling back, gingerly touching her swollen lip.

"Sorry, I—"

"Sshhh." Kitty smiled. Silently, she began unfastening the buttons on her dress, letting it finally fall to the floor.

Jimmy gasped as a kind of hopeful panic rose in him. "But I've never…"

"Sshhh," she repeated, leading him toward the bed. "I bet you'll figure it out."

18

J IMMY WATCHED FROM the window of his garret as a group of workmen disassembled the gallows that had plagued The Liberties for the past three weeks. He glanced nervously over his shoulder, but Kitty was still sleeping soundly. He approached the bed, the chair next to it creaking softly as he sat and watched her sleep. In his head, he went over the plan one more time. It could work—at least he hoped so.

No, he decided, it *must* work. He had to protect her. He might not be able to change the past, but he could determine the future.

Kitty sighed in her sleep and began to stir. Her eyes flicked open, momentarily startled before she realized where she was and relaxed. She smiled.

"Come here to me," she purred.

Jimmy let her envelop him. Let her kiss him, sensing her hunger.

"What time is it anyway?" she asked when she pulled

away, still sleepy.

"Almost nine o'clock, I think, but we'll know soon enough." He instinctively glanced in the direction of St. Catherine's Church.

She sat up. "That late already? We should get to work."

Jimmy noticed the 'we' in the sentence, and smiled. "Not today," he said, trying to summon the courage to make his proposal.

"Oh." She smiled mischievously and flopped back on the bed. "What have you got planned instead?"

He was tempted, for a moment, but he knew he must act, and act now. Kitty was fiercely independent. She had to be. But that meant that if he had any chance with this, he must be equally as bold. "There'll be plenty of time for that later," he said. "There's something I want to discuss with you first."

"Sounds serious," she said playfully.

Jimmy nodded.

That got her attention. She sat up, clutching the blanket to her chest. "If you have any regrets, now is the time—"

"I love you, Kitty."

She dropped the blanket as her hand flew to her mouth.

"I think I loved you from the first moment I set eyes on you."

"Jimmy…" Kitty's eyes watered.

His gaze flicked to her chest, and a shiver shot up his spine. He told himself to focus. "There's something I need to—"

She interrupted him with a kiss he was powerless to resist. "You've talked enough." Her body was warm where it pressed against him, and her forceful kiss pulled him down, toward the bed. Couldn't he allow himself one more moment of pleasure?

He drew back. "I need to… we need to—"

"Talking can wait." She kissed him again, even more fiercely, but he pulled himself free.

"For God's sake, Jimmy. What is it? Don't tell me you're having second thoughts."

"No," he protested. He stretched out a hand and tenderly brushed her cheek. "Of course not. But I do need to talk to you."

"What about?'

He cleared his throat, locking his eyes on hers. "Come to America with me."

"What?"

"You must come with me to America. I must take you away from all this. Protect you. Keep you safe."

Kitty gave him a peck on the nose. "It's sweet that you want to protect me, but I can look after myself." She leaned in to kiss him passionately again.

He held her away. "I'm serious," he insisted. "It's not safe for you here."

"I'm fine, Jimmy."

"How can you say that when you're taking risks like going up to the Castle and demanding that housekeeper's release?"

She clenched her jaw. "I see you've been talking to my uncle." Her eyes narrowed. "And the housekeeper has a name: Anne Devlin."

Jimmy pinched the bridge of his nose. "She has my sincerest sympathies, but you know as well as I do that the Castle will hold her as long as they see fit. It'll do her no good at all if you're sharing the next cell." He took a deep breath. "Look, I'm sorry for getting worked up. But I care about you, and I'm serious about America."

"I hear what you're saying," Kitty replied. "My uncle too." She threw her hands up. "You're both bloody right. But... I don't know. Is it too much to ask for someone else to care about this? I don't see anyone else volunteering to go up there in my place. Those bastards have held her for months now—without charge. The last time I was up there, they started spinning a new yarn, saying they had no record of her arrest or imprisonment." She shook her head. "I'm sick of it, Jimmy. They killed Robert Emmet. Thomas Russell is next. I'd give anything for it to be otherwise, but it's starting to look like the United Irishmen are finished. Despite everything we've suffered, the Crown's grip on Ireland is firmer than ever. What more do they want?"

"We can get away from all this, Kitty. The two of us. Together. We can start again in America. Leave all this behind."

She kissed his stubbled cheek. "Let's talk about this another time."

"No," he said, a little too sharply. "We have to talk about it now."

Her nose wrinkled. "Why now?"

"I've already decided. I'm leaving this Friday." He paused. "And you're coming with me."

Kitty's hand covered her mouth again.

"I can scrape together enough for a second ticket. We won't have to work off any contract. We'll be free."

"A second ticket?"

"I already have mine," he explained. "I bought it on Monday, before—"

"You can't just—"

"Listen, Kitty. We won't have much, but we'll have

each other. And our freedom. I have family in New York. My cousin Donal—you'll like him. We've been writing to each other since he went across a couple of years back. He's always telling me about all the opportunities over there, if you're willing to work hard."

"But…"

"No one there cares whether you're Catholic or Protestant. My father was a craftsman, not a market trader. But he soon found out that the Guild here have everything tied up in Dublin. Because he went to the wrong church, he couldn't practice his trade. Everything here is always limited by this shit. But our future can be different."

"Jimmy…"

"Imagine it, Kitty… just let yourself picture it for one moment. Land of our own. The freedom to do whatever we want. We could build a life there. Together." He tilted his chin down, staring at her expectantly from beneath his lowered brow.

When she spoke, eventually, it was in a low voice. "Sounds like you have it all figured out."

"Aye," he said. "I do."

"Except for one thing."

"What's that?"

"For fuck's sake, Jimmy. What about what *I* want?

You don't think I have hopes and dreams of my own? Or does my opinion not matter?" She let out a deep sigh.

"Well, I thought—"

"No, you didn't. You didn't think. You didn't think about what I might want. You just made this plan, like the big man, thinking I'd be the quiet little woman who nodded and followed." She jumped out of bed and rifled through the bedding, searching for her dress. When she found it, she shook it out and pulled it over her head. "Seeing as you're so full of grand schemes, what's your big idea now? What was your plan if I said no? You're going anyway, aren't you?"

Jimmy fell silent.

"I knew it," she sneered. "And what would happen next? Would you forget me? Or write me love letters to torment me? It looks like you never considered staying for me—not that I'd ever ask such a thing of you—but it's revealing that it never once crossed your mind." She scanned the room. "Where are my shoes?"

"Kitty, what are you doing?"

"What does it look like?"

"I don't know."

"Jesus, Jimmy, I'm leaving. Now where are my bloody shoes?" She put her hand on the doorknob. "Fine. Keep them. I'm still leaving. And don't you bother coming after me. If I don't see you again until I'm old and gray, that would still be too soon."

She slammed the door behind her.

19

NORA FUSSED AROUND him, making sure he'd packed all of Donal's presents safely. His mood was obvious, but his aunt must have assumed it sprang from doubt or fear. She kept assuring him that everything would be fine, that he shouldn't worry, that she'd write often and give him all the news from home. Jimmy didn't have the heart to tell her that his gloominess was caused by something else altogether.

For two days, his attempts to reach Kitty had ended in nothing but failure. After much cajoling and some outright pleading, Mahaffy had eventually agreed to pass on a message.

Her reply was quick in coming. "Tell him to fuck off to America."

Mahaffy also let him know, in very clear terms, that he was to push the matter no further. "I don't know what you said, or did," he warned, "but she's furious."

Jimmy forced a smile as he said his final goodbyes to

Nora and his cousins, and hoisted the cloth sack onto his shoulder. Nora had wanted to accompany him to the quays, but Jimmy talked her out of it. Luckily, she hadn't insisted. It was hard enough suppressing the voice that kept insisting he was making a terrible mistake. Kitty's rejection had scored him deeply. He'd been so sure she would jump at the chance of a fresh start with him that he'd acted like a fool. He knew that now, too late. His ship was leaving in two hours, and he was going to be aboard.

And that was that.

His final walk down Thomas Street was bittersweet. The gallows outside St. Catherine's Church were gone, but the railings had been festooned with green ribbons that fluttered madly over a blanket of candles and flowers—an impromptu shrine to Ireland's latest martyred son.

"It's amazing, isn't it?"

He turned to see Fergal Hayes.

"The Watch clear it away every evening, but the following morning it's back again. Proves that you can't kill it."

"Kill what?"

"Hope." Fergal grinned.

"I'm sorry for falling out with you." Jimmy put out his hand.

Fergal hesitated before shaking it. "I wasn't trying to come between the pair of ye."

"I know, I'm sorry."

He tipped his cap. "It's forgotten." He eyed Jimmy's cloth sack. "I guess it's true, then."

"She sails at four."

"You're doing the right thing," Fergal said. "It's going to get worse before it gets better."

"How can it get worse?"

He laughed. "They'll find a way." He embraced Jimmy, and then turned and began walking back to his stall. "Hey, Jimmy," he called. "Write to me."

"But you can't read!"

He winked. "I'll have to find a pretty girl who can."

Jimmy decided not to turn down Dirty Lane. He didn't want his last memory of Dublin to be the stench of the Liffey. Instead, he went up by Cornmarket, past Christchurch and that damned bar on Skinner's Row, and then continued by the Royal Exchange at Cork Hill until he reached Dame Street, beyond the Castle. The bottom of the street opened out into College Green, with the imposing Protestant splendor of Trinity opposite the old Irish Parliament building. Since Ireland's legislature voted itself out of existence four years beforehand, the site had been occupied by the Bank of Ireland.

"Sure, the moneymen really run the country anyway," Fergal had joked. Jimmy smiled at the memory, glad he'd the chance to mend one fence, at least.

He sighed as he walked up Hawkins Street to the river and saw the row of ship masts lining George's Quay. It took him some time to locate his own vessel, a little further down on Rogerson's Quay. There was little time to check the boat over. Jimmy was hustled aboard right away. He gazed forlornly at the quayside from the deck, wishing he'd had time to kiss the ground or say a short prayer—something—before being hurried up the gangplank, but it had all happened so quickly.

His throat constricted as the port side of the vessel began to fill with tearful emigrants, all waving handkerchiefs at loved ones down on the quay. *All of these people with their own hopes and dreams and disappointments. All these families and separated lovers, wondering if they'll ever lay eyes on each other once more.* It made his heart ache.

He walked over to the other side, blinking away tears, pushing down the thoughts he wouldn't allow himself to think. He couldn't—not until they cast anchor and set sail. Every couple of minutes, a wail went up from one of the departing passengers, despair at finally realizing there was no going back. Jimmy chewed his nails to the quick and searched for a distraction.

Seagulls hovered above the boat, not even needing to flap their wings. He gazed out at the Northside. It was almost as foreign a land to him as America, but then, Dublin had always felt like two cities unhappily married by a river. Sure, you had to go as far upstream as Capel Street before you could cross to the other bank. He remembered what Da used to say: a city designed for carriages, not people.

Da also said the Northside used to be the posh side of the river, with the wealthiest Protestants giving their family names to the grand stretches housing ostentatious new homes. But as soon as the Fitzgeralds struck out to the south and built Kildare House, the winds of fashion brought the rest across soon after. They abandoned those newly built houses for yet grander affairs. Now, St. Stephen's Green—a former gallows he'd visited with his father many years before, where Da had shared the story of Darkey Kelley—was the desired address for the well-heeled.

He shook his head. Da had been fascinated by the case—along with the broadsheet writers. It wasn't hard to see why. Darkey Kelly once ran the famous Maiden Tower brothel. Although the brothel was down in Hell, it was a slightly more upmarket establishment than the usual and was often frequented by the gentry. It was also well known that Darkey provided entertainment at the more salubrious addresses of those who simply couldn't be seen wandering Dublin's saucier parts. The most salacious rumors claimed that Darkey and her girls were part of the notorious Hell Fire club. One of those members was the City Sherriff's son, who had, apparently, made Darkey pregnant. Desperate to avoid a scandal that could ruin his prospects, he pressured her to give up the baby and she reluctantly made a deposit in the foundling wheel outside St. Aubergh's church, like so many girls who'd worked for her over the years. But after she'd abandoned her child to its destiny, he had Darkey Kelly arrested for the babe's murder. Of course, she couldn't produce the infant in her defense.

Some said the whores of Copper Alley had rioted for two straight days after Darkey's hanging, raging against the abuse of power that had ended their madam. Peace wasn't restored until the Watch took possession of her brothel and shut down the bar. After the Watchmen helped themselves to the last of the stock—for safety's sake, of course—thoughts turned to the brothel-keeper's stash. A woman like Darkey was bound to have money hidden somewhere. The crowbars came out, and the place was torn apart. They didn't find any money, but they did find six dead men buried under her floorboards.

As Da used to say, Darkey Kelly may not have been a witch, but she surely was a killer.

Jimmy shook his head. It was like a tale from one of Da's old books, before he and Ma had been forced to sell them all. He almost laughed at the thought that he was now starring in an adventure of his own—well, if this ship would ever bloody cast off. He fantasized about being a man of wealth or importance, someone who could hold sway with the captain, storm the fo'c'sle, and demand their departure. He placed a finger inside his waistband, checking on his money pouch, and for an awful moment thought it had been pinched by some guttersnipe. But it had merely slipped down a touch, he realized, rearranging the straps furtively. It contained his only possessions of any value: the rest of his guineas, his old map of The Colonies, and Da's wedding ring. The rest was replaceable.

Sadness gripped him as he realized he had no memento of Kitty. The questioning voice returned once more, this time less willing to be dismissed so easily. He returned to the port side to distract himself, just as the captain gave the order to cast off. He gripped the rail, fighting the overwhelming urge to charge down the gangplank, to march up Thomas Street and take his place beside Fergal and the other traders, to find Kitty and beg her forgiveness.

He gritted his teeth.

The gangplank creaked and lurched as it was raised, and Jimmy watched as sailors crawled up the rigging to unfurl the grand sails. The vessel seemed to twitch, to sway a little, and then to slowly ease itself from the quay wall. Emigrants wiped away their tears and put on their bravest faces, as if waving all the more furiously could dispel all their doubts. He paced to the stern and back again, resisting the urge to scream. He stared down at the dark, dirty water, at the quay slowly slipping away.

Damn it anyway.

He tested the weight of the sack in his hand. It was heavy enough, but it felt like nothing as he hurled it with all his strength over the port side of the ship, ignoring the cries of surprise as it sailed over the heads of his fellow passengers and flew towards the dock. Before anyone had a chance to stop him, Jimmy hurried into the center of the boat, measured the distance to the prow, and then sped towards it. Jumping at the last moment, he launched himself off the guardrail with the ball of his foot. And then he was in the air, springing clear of the boat, not even crying out—until he remembered he couldn't swim.

He hit the water with a noisy splash before submerging, fast. The extra weight of his clothes dragged him down and he panicked, trying to wrench off his boots, but they were stuck fast. Unbearable pressure bit into his lungs, and he gasped, his mouth filling with the Liffey until everything went black.

20

H E HEAVED THE Liffey's foul waters up from his guts and onto the quayside flagstones. His throat was raw with retching, and he wiped a long trail of slime from his mouth.

"He's alive!" someone cried, which was a relief—because he felt like death. His vision gradually came into focus. First, he saw a moustache. Then a pleasantly rotund face, leaning in.

"You're some feckin' eejit," the man said, and dropped a dripping wet sack beside his head. "I believe this is yours—or what's left of it."

Jimmy retched once more.

"Sit up," suggested the man.

"I'm grand," he gasped. "Just need a minute." Jimmy slowly got to his feet, leaning on the hirsute man for support.

"The Watch are coming. Unless you want to get locked up, you better scarper."

Jimmy thanked him and stumbled up Moss Street. Once he was far enough away from the quays, he sat down to take stock. All that was left was a sodden loaf of bread. Suddenly alarmed, his hand fumbled with his waistband, but, miraculously, his pouch was still in place.

Well, that was stupid, he thought, shivering. He stood and coughed up a glob of salty phlegm. Abandoning his sack, he made his way towards The Liberties, leaving wet footprints half the way to College Green.

He soon realized he'd made an awful mistake coming this way. He was attracting the wrong kind of attention from the rich types perambulating around the giant statue of King Billy. His nervousness mounted as he passed, but they gave him a wide berth, tugging on each other's arms and grumbling behind their hands. He must have been some sight; his bare feet and wet clothes amidst all that satin and lace. Not wanting to attract the Watch, Jimmy snatched up a worn, filthy blanket some beggar chased away from Trinity must have discarded on the pavement. He wrapped it around his shoulders as if it were a second skin, affecting a limp and a wheezing cough that would keep anyone away. Dragging his left foot behind him, as if powerless to control it, he paused every few steps to hack up his lungs. Soon, the wealthy eyes began to skip right over him—which suited his needs perfectly.

He continued this way up Dame Street until he reached the Castle entrance, where a lone voice was haranguing the guards. A lone, familiar voice.

He turned. Kitty.

Jimmy drew the cloak over his face and hurried past, his heart thumping. What else could he do?

Once out of sight, he stopped to think. He had to get her away from there, but how? It was only a matter of time before she was recognized. That blasted bar on Skinner's Row was just around the corner. If its prices were anything to go by, it was likely packed out every day with Castle workers: sergeants, clerks, lawyers working for the administration. Kitty was taking a terrible risk.

Jimmy pondered his options. Just limping up and hauling her away was no good. He'd been there that night too, after all. And he was pretty sure the Castle wouldn't believe his claims of innocence. While he was thinking, he heard Kitty's voice ratchet up another notch.

"I will not step away," she spat.

He crept back to get a look.

One of the soldiers lunged towards her, but she leaned backward out of reach. "Arrest her!" demanded the sergeant.

He searched the street for something to distract them. A broken cobble a few yards back might do; he scooped it up, keeping one eye on the guards. They hadn't even noticed him. He weighed the stone in his hand. It felt just right. He trained his eye on the sergeant who was barking orders and pointing at Kitty. Realizing her error at last, she was slowly backing away.

With a cry, he lobbed the cobble towards the soldiers, hoping to distract them long enough for Kitty to escape, knowing it was imperative they chase him instead. The soldiers turned his direction as the stone sailed through the air. The sergeant pointed at Jimmy. "Seize that—"

His order was cut short by the cobble striking him square on the forehead. He flopped forwards onto the ground.

The soldiers stood back for a moment, shocked. Jimmy let his cloak fall to the ground and Kitty's eyes widened in recognition. "Oh, shit," she said.

"Run!" he screamed, his own feet fixed to the spot only through a supreme effort of willpower. His muscles twitched, eager to sprint away to freedom, but he knew that he must delay as long as possible. It was her only chance to get away.

The soldiers closed the distance. Behind them, more

poured out of the gate. Still Jimmy waited … and waited. And then, finally, he ran.

He gathered speed, pounding down Essex Street before banking sharply into Copper Alley, keeping up a tremendous pace even while he bounded up the Forty Steps into High Street. Up ahead, he could see Kitty racing towards Cutpurse Lane and Thomas Street. He needed to buy her more time. Peering back over his shoulder, he saw the first soldiers pouring out of the mouth of the Forty Steps, and he tore down Back Lane towards Patrick's Street, all the while roaring threats at the soldiers to ensure they followed him.

The road was quiet, which was not good for him. But he had to press on. If he turned right, down Hanover Lane or Limerick Alley, he might lose them in the warren behind The Coombe, but he could just as easily run right into them too. He needed to lure them in the opposite direction until Kitty was clear. Jimmy cut left instead, racing through the grounds of the cathedral and skidding onto Kevin's Street, just opposite the Cabbage Gardens. Dropping breathlessly to a normal pace, he blended into the crowd outside the Archbishop's Palace.

He kept his head down and strode over to the corner of Golden Lane. Taking the turn onto Bull Alley, glancing over his shoulder for his pursuers, he walked smack into a soldier.

The Englishman grabbed Jimmy by the shoulders. "Watch where you're going!" he warned, shoving him firmly away. Then the soldier simply turned on his heel and stalked off.

Jimmy couldn't believe his luck. He was still standing there, glued to the spot like an idiot, when the soldier reached the other side of the street and casually glanced over his shoulder. His nose wrinkled at the sight of Jimmy, standing stock-still. The Englishman opened his mouth to speak, but a whistle sounded and a company of men charged up Golden Lane.

Jimmy bolted.

He cut across Patrick Street and Francis Street, and then little Spittal Square. He was getting closer, but he could hear the soldiers closing in. His legs were beginning to tire. If he could just make it to Lark Street, he could clamber over the back wall and take refuge in Nora's yard. His calves burned. His feet turned to lead. He pumped his legs as hard as he could, but he wasn't quick enough to pull clear. The soldiers began reeling him in. His smooth gait started to falter, his muscles flagging, his breath coming in ragged gasps. Nora's back wall was in the distance, but he already knew he wouldn't make it. And when they finally tackled him to the ground, it was almost a relief.

21

H E DIDN'T FEEL like a hero. His trial had none of the drama of Robert Emmet's two months beforehand, and he was afforded no opportunity to give a speech or have his thoughts recorded for posterity—not that he would have known what to say.

He was guilty, that much he could accept. It wasn't any great shock when the judge gave him seven years. All the others before him on that day had received the same sentence. A team of cattle rustlers from Ballybrack, an egg thief from Goatstown, a couple of chalkers from Howth, and a shifty-looking fella from Raheny who went down for savagely beating his wife—seven years apiece, all of them. And they would all be transported to the new penal colony at Van Diemen's Land to serve out their sentences.

Jimmy spent his days curled into a ball in Kilmainham Gaol, once again on a straw mattress, although considerably more rancid than the one he used to sleep on.

In the days leading up to his trial, the turnkey had taunted him mercilessly, telling him that he was housed in Robert Emmet's old cell. "And you know what happened to him," he would sneer, dragging a dirty thumbnail across his throat.

It was a convincing threat. The hanging didn't stop after the rebel leader's death. One man even tasted the noose in the yard, right outside Jimmy's cell. But this prick of a guard had spun the same yarn for all the prisoners, and it had been especially effective on the day of Emmet's execution, when his headless corpse was paraded in the courtyard of Kilmainham Gaol for all the prisoners to see. Had he shared the same cell as Emmet? He would never know. Not that it mattered, but these little details plagued him. Perhaps, he supposed, it was a way for his mind to focus on something else, something other than the morbid fate that had been carved out for him. *I got what I wanted,* he thought with some bitterness. *I'm leaving Ireland.*

The only respite from his unending horror was the knowledge he'd saved Kitty. Or so he had to assume. No one came to visit. No one passed him a message, no matter how many he tried to send out. But if he didn't assume she was safe, he'd go mad. Absently, he wondered whether Auntie Nora knew he was in a cell just down the road, rather than on a ship halfway to America.

Letting out a primal howl he fell back on the mattress, squeezing his eyes, trying to force himself to cry. But even that small relief was denied him.

"Keep it down, or you won't get your visitor."

Jimmy jumped up and darted across the room, slamming into the grate. "Visitor? What visitor?" But the turnkey was already gone, out of view.

He's playing with me again, Jimmy decided, swearing to not let the bastard get to him. He recalled his last meeting with Fergal, his words about hope, and he realized bitterly that hope could also be used as a weapon. These last two months, waiting to be sent to the other side of the world, had been pure torture. The guards had lied to him throughout, promising the departure was set for the next day, then the next week; at one point, they even claimed transportation had been postponed indefinitely and that a reprieve could be on the cards. All for sport.

Jimmy stopped himself from pounding on the door. What if it's true? He paced his cell again, deciding he was being toyed with. It was not enough for the cat to simply kill the mouse. He punched the stone wall instead, leaving bloody fist prints on whitewashed bricks.

When a key rattled in the door, he didn't even bother turning around, not wanting to let the guards see his torment.

"Jimmy," he heard. "Oh, Jimmy."

That voice.

He rubbed his eyes in disbelief and sprang to his feet. Kitty closed the space between them.

"Hands off," the turnkey warned.

Jimmy ignored him, hugging her tighter, but she wriggled free and nodded at the guard—who stepped outside and slammed the door. "Remember, I'm watching," he shouted through the grille. "You only have a couple of minutes."

"We don't have long," Kitty said. "And I won't be allowed to visit you again. They're not letting anyone in."

"How did you—?"

"It doesn't matter. Just listen: there's something I need to tell you." She stared at him strangely. "Well, two things."

He was glad to see she was looking healthy. Her hair had been cut short—presumably so she wouldn't be recognized—and she had put on a little weight. It suited her; she had been too thin before. Her eyes, though—fierce, challenging, almost mocking—they hadn't changed one bit.

"Go on," he said.

"I'm sorry, Jimmy. I'm sorry this happened to you." She began sobbing.

He stepped forward to comfort her, but the guard rapped on the door. "Keep back!"

Kitty stepped away. "Listen to me go on." She wiped a tear from her face. "Talking like I had nothing to do with it." She eyed the door nervously.

Jimmy shook his head, and she nodded, understanding his warning.

"I should have said yes," she continued. "I should have gone with you." She bowed her head. "I was a fool. If only I hadn't been so proud…"

"I love you just as you are."

She looked up, her face contorted with pain.

"I'll always love you," he continued. His eyes flicked to the door. "They haven't beaten me. I'll find a way home." He spread his bloodied hands. "Somehow, I'll do it. I promise you."

"Don't…"

He remembered her touch, her naked body beneath him, her eyes glittering like jewels as they made love. "I'll come back," he promised once more. "And I'll find you."

"You can't say that," she cried. "You can't make that promise."

"I can."

Her face flushed red. "No one ever comes back."

"I will, damn it."

"And what am I supposed to do? Wait?"

He was lost for words. Of course he couldn't ask her to wait. He clenched his jaw.

"I'm sorry, Jimmy."

He bit his cheek. "What will you do?"

She smiled in response, and the tears spilled down her cheeks. "I suppose I'll get married," she said. "I won't want to, of course, but it will be expected of me. So I'll do it." She stared at the ceiling for a moment, and then met Jimmy's stare. "And I suppose I'll have children too. That's what is expected of a dutiful wife. But I'll—"

The door wheezed and scraped and clattered as the guard wrestled it open.

"One more minute, please, I beg you." She placed a hand on the turnkey's forearm. "If you have any heart at all—"

The guard grabbed her wrist and wrenched her towards him. Jimmy let out a cry and pounced. But in his weakened state, the guard was able to fell him with two quick blows. He threw Kitty out the door and shouted an order to his men waiting outside. Then he gave Jimmy a taste of his boot. Jimmy's last thought, before he passed out, made him laugh through bloodied teeth: I should have fucking kissed her.

22

SIX WEEKS LATER, on a cold December morning just before Christmas, Jimmy stood silently on Bachelor's Walk, along with eighty other men whose hands and feet were chained together, waiting to board the vessel. He wondered how long it would take to get to Van Diemen's Land. They hadn't been told anything at all. For weeks, rumors had filled the prison that war with France was taking its toll and England couldn't spare the ships to send them to the other side of the world. The more optimistic in Kilmainham Gaol thought this might lead to a general amnesty, like after the '98 Rebellion, but Jimmy knew deep down that life wasn't done kicking him in the guts.

They slowly shuffled towards the gangplank. It was the first time Jimmy had been out of his cell since his incarceration, and he breathed deeply, closing his eyes so he could quit staring at the name painted so brightly on the hull of the vessel that was to be his home for the next six months—if he survived that long.

The crowd watching the procession was largely silent. Jimmy scanned the faces for anyone he knew: Kitty, Nora, Fergal, even Mahaffy, but he saw no one he recognized. *There goes my chance of a heroic escape*, he thought, rubbing where the manacles had cut into his wrists. Gallows humor was all he had left, and the thought almost made him chuckle. A line of British soldiers stood proud and firm in their blood-colored coats, eyeing the crowd with menace, almost daring them to try something. But the people watching seemed resigned to what was happening. Only the young failed to understand that there was no hope left, nothing to fight for anymore. A boy of six or seven screamed for his father. *Poor sod,* thought Jimmy. The little waif wrestled free from his mother's grasp. "Da!" he screamed, darting for the line of convicts.

Jimmy watched as the boy skillfully evaded one soldier, and then the next.

"Da!" the boy yelled again. Curiously, the child headed right for him. *A feint*, he decided. He barreled into Jimmy's legs, wailing. "Da, don't leave. Please. Don't go."

His fellow prisoners looked on with mute pity. Soldiers grabbed the boy and dragged him away. Jimmy said nothing, just continued shuffling towards the gangplank. The line was moving faster now, presumably to avoid further dramatics.

As he stepped onto the gangplank, Jimmy felt something chafe against his skin, something rough. He glanced from side to side. When he was sure no one was looking, he slipped his thumb into his waistband. Paper, he could feel it now. That boy must have slipped it to him. A note? For the first time in weeks, he felt the teasing tickle of hope. Feverish with curiosity, he had to counsel himself to remain calm as he carefully shuffled up the gangplank. He could feel the note slipping from his waistband. He'd lost far too much weight in that cell. Each step was pure torture as the paper slipped further. Once he reached the deck, he saw what had been taking so long. An officer seated at a table was questioning the prisoners before they were unshackled and led into the belly of the ship. "Name?" The officer didn't even look up.

"Jimmy O'Flaherty."

He traced his finger down the page until he found the entry he was looking for and placed a tick next to it. His eyes narrowed. He looked up, smiling briefly at Jimmy before beckoning one of his men over. He tapped the page beside Jimmy's name, and the soldier nodded.

Jimmy didn't know what that meant exactly, but he figured it was nothing good. The guards leered at him, but he resolved to ignore their cheap provocation.

Still rubbing his wrists after the manacles were removed, Jimmy was led down steep stairs into a large chamber below deck. It took a moment for his eyes to adjust to the darkness—the only illumination coming from the open hatches above. Men lined both sides of the room, each shackled to a loop on a long bar. His heart sank.

He numbly followed as the guard chained him to a spare loop on the rail, taking stock of his new companions as he passed them. Some were clearly mad, gabbling, flagellating themselves, their straining eyes darting back-and-forth. Others were coiled, watching the soldiers, waiting for an opportunity to pounce. Newly convicted, Jimmy guessed. Most kept to themselves, massaging their ankles or taking the opportunity to sit down. Many stared back at him with what looked like sympathy.

That puzzled Jimmy greatly, until he remembered the boy on the quay. They must have thought it was his son, and these men must be leaving family behind themselves.

Seven years.

He pushed the thought out of his mind as the last

prisoner was brought down and tethered to the wall like a truculent goat. Finally, he took the opportunity to discreetly draw the paper from his waistband. An officer started to announce the regulations governing their voyage, but Jimmy had trouble focusing on his words. He was desperate to read the note, which was now clenched in his fist. Only one part caught his attention: if the prisoners respected the rules, the officers may permit them to be unchained. And if their behavior was exemplary, they may even be allowed up on deck for short periods of exercise.

The officer's face hardened. "If you break the rules," he said, "you'll soon find we have plenty more ways of punishing you than leaving you chained up all day. Unless you enjoy the taste of the whip, you'll heed this warning." He drew his lips together into a thin line. "I trust I've made myself clear."

He turned on his heel and stomped back up the stairs. Finally, once he was sure no other soldiers were coming, Jimmy unclenched his fist and smoothed out the mysterious paper. The light was too dim where he was stationed. He couldn't quite make out the writing, but he could tell it was a letter. He leaned towards the staircase, hoping to catch a little more light.

"What are you up to?"

Jimmy turned to see one prisoner watching him, bemused. He waved the letter. "Trying to read this."

"Might've been better to catch up on your correspondence before today," the man said with a broken-toothed grin. "Conditions are hardly ideal."

Jimmy forced a smile in return, hoping this was someone he could trust. "I'm only after getting it."

"Ah." The man tapped his nose. "So that's what the little snot was up to. Very good," he said. "Very good indeed."

Jimmy peered at the letter in his hand, wondering if he'd ever get to read the bloody thing. But the friendly prisoner took the hint and turned away. Then the column of light moved.

At first, Jimmy thought it was a miracle, that he was bending the beam of light through sheer force of will. But he soon realized the ship was tacking. The beam swung one way and then the next, and he unfolded the letter and stretched as far as his manacles would allow. Finally, the light traveled in his direction, frustratingly slowly at first, but then gathering speed as the vessel did. He positioned himself to catch it, but the beam of light passed over him too fast. He was only able to glance at the very first words, right at the top. It was a letter all right, even if the salutation it opened with was:

"You're a feckin' eejit."

The light danced cruelly away, but he smiled none-theless. For it was Kitty. A moment later, his luck returned. The light moved towards him and held position. He stretched out and continued reading.

"You didn't let me finish. What I wanted to say was this: You can't ask me to wait seven years. You just can't. I could make that promise, and I'd mean it. But seven years is a long time to be crying every day, tearing your hair out over someone who you don't know is alive or dead, let alone coming home. I will cry. And I'll do it for a long time, believe me. Because I love you, Jimmy O'Flaherty."

The next couple of words were smudged by what looked like a teardrop. But he could make out the second half of the sentence. "…but some day I'll stop. And I'll marry someone because I can't take the feeling anymore. I'll have children, because that's what's expected of a dutiful wife. I'll live in one of those dreadful, white-washed cottages miles from anywhere. And by the time you finally get your arse back here, I'll be so bloody bored that I'll happily run away with you."

She ended with a simple: "Love, Kitty."

Jimmy stared at the final words for some time before folding the letter and placing it into his shirt pocket. The ship creaked as it turned into the wind and filled its sails. He could hear prisoners chattering at the other end of the chamber, speculating about the temper of the guards and the conditions they could expect in Van Diemen's Land. He thought of Kitty. One hand on his breast pocket, he swore he would make it home, whatever it took.

And then he lay back and dreamed of Ireland.

Acknowledgements

I started with only a vague sense of wanting to explore Robert Emmet's much overlooked Rising in 1803. History class in school didn't devote too much attention to it; at the time it was considered a bit of a fool's errand, and it is only subsequent scholarship that has given it greater importance and placed it in the fuller context of Irish history. Unlike my previous books, I didn't focus on the historical protagonists. This time I decided to come at it from street level, viewing the action from the perspective of someone who is, perhaps, a little more ambivalent about it all.

Patrick Power, Irial Glynn, and Niall Cummins gave very useful reading suggestions and research tips at this stage. *Liberty Boy* could have gone in any direction from there but I was drawn to the idea of basing it around Thomas Street in Dublin. Out of a huge reading pile, two books were essential to understanding the United Irishmen and Robert Emmet: Marianne Elliot's *Robert Emmet: The Making of a Legend*, and, particularly, *Robert Emmet and the Rising of 1803* by Ruan O'Donnell. A fascinating radio show from Claremorris Community Radio called *Irish Heroes, Poets and Villains* introduced me to chilling figure known colloquially as The Walking Gallows and also detailed other horrendous excess of the Militia in 1798, which loomed so large afterwards. (I also pinched from them the striking George Nugent Reynolds which opens this book.) *What The Epaulets Were For* by author Colm Tóibín, which appeared in the Autumn 2003 issue of *Dublin Review*, is an excellent overview of Robert Emmet's legacy. And a number of articles in *History Ireland* magazine were of significant help in untangling the more impenetrable aspects of the period, especially one published in the July/August 2005 issue by Adrian Hardiman (who passed away recently) entitled *The Show Trial of Robert Emmet*—which made sense of Emmet's conflicting motivations, and explained how his defence counsel was a spy in the employ of Dublin Castle.

The Liberty and Ormond Boys gave great insight into the factional and agrarian violence of the time, and its author James Kelly kindly answered questions by email. *John Rocque's Dublin: A Guide to the Georgian City* by Colm Lennon and John Montague was crucial for getting around the warren of streets which made up The Liberties, and *The Liberties: A History* by Maurice Curtis gave a wonderful sense of the people which inhabited them. However, the most comprehensive resource in terms of Dublin's social history was the endlessly entertaining blog *Come Here To Me*.

I'd like to thank the little production team that has been with me from the start: Karin Cox did another excellent job with the editing and Kate Gaughran created a beautiful cover. Fellow writers Libbie Hawker and Michael Wallace read early drafts of the story and gave me some great suggestions to improve it. Of course, any errors that remain are entirely my own. I would also like to thank my family and friends back home for their continual support, particularly my parents Mary & Benny Gaughran. And, since I've been living Prague, the Vostrovskýs have shown me great kindness and hospitality for which I'll always be grateful.

Finally, I'd like to thank Ivča for being a sounding board for all of the ideas in this book, and plenty which didn't make it too; for reading early chapters and giving constant encouragement; for helping me figure out thorny plot points; and for supporting me the whole way through, even when I was being pretty damn unbearable.

This one's for you.

About the Author

David M. Gaughran is Irish but lives in Portugal these days, somewhere north of Lisbon in a lovely little fishing village. He likes dogs, whiskey, collecting old records, laborious puns, and also cooking elaborate feasts and inviting exactly nobody around to share them. He is also fond of slow cars, fast walks on the beach, movies which contain some form of time-loop, and any kind of song with a call-and-response element. When not busy learning everything he can about guillotines, he writes historical adventures like *Liberty Boy*, *Mercenary*, and *A Storm Hits Valparaiso*, as well as science fiction and writer guides under another name. Visit **DavidGaughran Books.com** to get a free novel. "Sure, why not?" says you.

David runs a monthly newsletter for readers where you get exclusive discounts and sneak peeks at upcoming books, as well as all sorts of fascinating stories from history which didn't quite make it into books. Yet. He is busy working on *Diemen's Land* and you will get an automatic email when it's launched if you sign up at **DavidGaughranBooks.com**.

You will also find links there to Facebook and Book-Bub and all the other places where you can connect with David. And you can also send him an email via the site; he reads every message and responds to everything personally. Finally, word-of-mouth is crucial for any author to succeed. If you enjoyed the book, please consider leaving a review online. Even if it's only a line or two, it would be a *huge* help and David would greatly appreciate it.

Made in the USA
Columbia, SC
27 November 2022